Righting Wrongs

By: Cristina Grenier

ISBN 13: 978-1-63156-028-6

Righting Wrongs

TABLE OF CONTENTS

Table of Contents 2

Publishers Notes 3

CHAPTER 1 - Difficulties 4

CHAPTER 2 - Changes 23

CHAPTER 3 - Trial By Fire 37

CHAPTER 4 - Close Encounters 54

CHAPTER 5 - Secrets 73

CHAPTER 6 - Change 90

CHAPTER 7 - Reality 111

CHAPTER 8 - Fracture 137

CHAPTER 9 - Righting Wrongs 153

About The Author 164

Cristina Grenier

PUBLISHERS NOTES

Disclaimer

This is a work of fiction. Names, characters, businesses, places, events and incidents are either the products of the author's imagination or used in a fictitious manner. Any resemblance to actual persons, living or dead, or actual events is purely coincidental.

Paperback Edition

Manufactured in the United States of America

CHAPTER 1 - DIFFICULTIES

"Xaviar?" Cece peered up the dark staircase with a frown before checking her watch. It was nearly seven o'clock, which meant that the boy *should* be getting dressed and ready for school. Somehow, however, she doubted that he had even stumbled from bed yet. Such was the lot of teenagers. Literal force was required to get them to do anything.

Groaning, she hitched up the hem of her robe and started up the stairs. She had bought the garment at a thrift shop in Harlem years ago and though it was far too big for her, it was thick enough to keep out the winter chill. The quality was necessary when one lived in an apartment as drafty as the small two bedroom she rented in south Brooklyn.

She pushed the cracked door to her brother's room open, a scowl coloring her face. As she'd expected, the young man was still sawing off beneath a mountain of blankets, his alarm clock blaring away aimlessly. Rolling her eyes, Cece crossed the room to yank each separate covering from Xaviar's sleeping form, one by one. It took her an astounding five layers to reach the boy, and once he was exposed, he merely groaned, shifting in the bed.

"M'sleepy." Turning over, he attempted to bury his face in the pillows – just before Cece snatched them away.

"Wake *up* Xaviar! You have to be out the door for school in twenty minutes!" Her shrill tone had her brother bolting upright, his hazel eyes wide and bleary.

"Shit!"

"Watch your mouth." Cece warned him sharply. Regardless of his state of consciousness, she wasn't going to have him using that kind of language under her roof. With a low, tortured groan, the tall boy raised his arms above his head in a languid stretch that made Cece want to throw his alarm clock at his head. "Boy, get out the bed!"

"Ugh..." Xaviar rubbed long fingered hands roughly over

his face. "Cece, I'm sick. I can't go to school today." He flopped back down against the bed, clutching his stomach in mock pain. "It hurts..."

Cece merely crossed her arms over her chest, cocking her hip as she glared down at the young man. She'd been seeing through his fibs since he was in diapers. It was really astounding how he thought he could still fool her after fourteen years.

"You are *not* sick, Xaviar. You ate three double cheeseburgers with fries last night. That's not a sick man's meal."

"But my stomach hurts *now*," He whined, peering up at her through his fingers. "I think I ate too much last night..."

Cece's eyes narrowed. "Xaviar Jamal Thompson, if you do not stop telling stories and get up this instant, *I* will eat your poptarts. *And* take ten dollars off your allowance this week."

That did the trick. Xaviar bolted upright, his hand leaving his stomach almost immediately as he slithered from the bed to the floor to hunt for his sneakers. When Cece only arched a brow at his miraculous recovery, he shot her a sheepish smile. "I feel better all of a sudden."

"Yeah, I'll bet you do." Shaking her head in exasperation, Cece left the room to pad back down the drafty staircase, pulling her robe tight around her. Her brother was a horror to get out of bed in the morning, and had been ever since he'd reached adolescence. As a child, he leapt from bed at eight AM every day, begging her to watch cartoons with him or to take him to the park on weekends. How a few years changed a growing boy.

But Xaviar wasn't the only one who'd changed.

Frowning, Cece glanced around the ramshackle apartment they'd moved into half a year ago. The ceiling was swollen and bulging from water damage, you could hear termites in the walls, and the cabinets in the kitchen were fairly falling off the hinges. For this, she paid over $1000 a month.

New York was New York, she supposed. But recently, the Big Apple had dealt her some painful blows. After tirelessly working for a fashion organization that had hired her right out of school for seven years, she'd been laid off unexpectedly. Not only did she lose the job she loved, but also the steady income that went with it. In the city, making it was difficult even in the best of times.

These were certainly not the best of times.

Cece was living off her savings, but even those were starting to run thin. She'd been looking for jobs in her field for what seemed like an eternity, but positions in the fashions industry were like ghosts: hard to find and even harder to keep. She'd been lucky to land the position she had straight out of school. But she hadn't understood how lucky until she'd tried to look for a new one. Now, she was trying to support a child on five hundred dollars a week, out of which came their groceries, gas for her car, funds for anything Xaviar might need at school, and emergency transportation. It was a tight budget for the big apple, and Cece was having more than a little trouble making ends meet.

She needed to find work, and she needed to do it fast. They'd last perhaps a few more months without a stable source of income.

Leaning against the yellowing counter in the kitchen, she took a bite of the single poptart she allowed herself for breakfast. It hadn't always been like this. A year ago, she'd felt as if she'd had the world at her feet. She and Xaviar had been living in a nice place in Harlem, and there'd been more than enough money for food and occasional nights out. Cece hadn't thought her life could get much better.

Xaviar was a good kid. Despite the fact that she knew he must desire a father figure in his life, she'd done the best she could with him. She'd been faced with the decision of taking him in or allowing him to be shuffled into the foster system when she was only eighteen. Of course, she hadn't been able to fathom letting her own flesh and blood go to someone else when she could take care of him, so she'd taken on the hard task of raising a child when she was still one herself.

It had been hard. She'd worked two jobs all the way through college, changed thousands of diapers, and always made sure that Xaviar was fed before she was. He was a happy baby, always smiling and laughing, totally unaware of the existence of his father or the man's controversial identity. All Cece ever wanted was to keep it that way but she knew she owed him more. When he turned six, she had told him exactly who his father was, and where he was, giving him the option to get to know the man.

    She herself wanted nothing more to do with Jamal Thompson. He'd made her childhood a living hell after her mother had died, and it seemed like she'd suffered from the consequences of his actions for her entire life. To her relief, however, Xaviar showed no interest in the man who'd given him up. Even more amazingly, he seemed to want more than anything to be the antithesis of his father; and when he'd been attending special classes for the gifted when they were in Harlem, Cece had known that he would be nothing like Jamal.

    Now, doubt had begun to creep in.

    Xaviar was now zoned to some piece of shit institution where the students were more concerned with trying to sneak weapons in than actually educating themselves. Though she knew her brother was smart, Cece couldn't help but fear that his surroundings might have some impact on him. It wasn't that she thought Xaviar would ever pick up a gun, but she feared that perhaps other, less obvious temptations would begin to appeal to him. Alcohol, drugs, gambling, petty theft...the list went on and on.

    Being a parent was the most complicated and most rewarding thing she'd ever endeavored towards in her life. Though she had shed tears and cursed her father on bad days, most of the time, she was glad that Jamal had never really gotten his claws into his son. The results could only have been damaging for Xaviar.

    However, in their current situation, she found herself struggling to do better. They lived in a shitty neighborhood with shitty schools and her efforts to escape it were exhausting. Her girlfriends frequently told her that she needed to take a break – to go out and live a little with them on Friday nights. They encouraged her to take a break from parenting – to find a date, get

Righting Wrongs

laid, and soothe her stress away.

Her funds simply wouldn't allow it, and though they had offered to pay, she was too proud to accept their money. There had been a time where she'd had no problem funding her chosen lifestyle. Xaviar hadn't had to sleep in a freezing room and he'd come home to dinner on the table every day. She'd had her fair share of dates with men both attractive and attentive, though none of them had kept her interest for long. Those times would return. She just had to get through the trying ones first.

"Time?"

She turned, startled, as Xaviar hurtled down the stairs at the speed of light, clad in dirty jeans and a hoodie. Cece forced herself to bite her tongue – she couldn't very well reprimand him for dressing in dirty clothes when they didn't have laundry facilities. She herself would have to gather laundry to haul to the laundry mat later.

God, she missed having her own washer and dryer.

"It's quarter to eight. Please tell me you're ready to get out the door." She popped the last bite of her poptart into her mouth as Xaviar grabbed the glass of orange juice she'd set out for him and chugged it.

"I'm good to go." He set his empty glass down on the counter with a clatter before taking up his two poptarts, one in each hand. For a moment, Cece allowed herself to appreciate her brother's departure from the style of the neighborhood. His pants didn't sag, and though he wore a long sleeved shirt, at least it was mostly clean and ironed. His bright hazel eyes concentrated on his food as he tore through the two pastries she'd warmed for him and, for a moment and she couldn't help but smile. He was the image of their father, from caramel colored skin to closely buzzed dark curls; but she knew that Xaviar was completely different. It was almost as if he could single-handedly banish bad memories of Jamal from her mind.

Quickly, she slipped on her snow boots and took off her robe, shivering in the jeans and t-shirt she wore beneath. It couldn't be more than forty degrees in the apartment, and she could only afford to turn on the heat in the evenings when Xaviar came home. She spent a moment hunting for her coat, only to see her brother holding it out to her with a mischievous smile.

"Looking for this?"

Rolling her eyes, Cece returned the gesture, pleased when he offered to slip the coat onto her arms. She'd taught him to respect women from a young age, and he seemed to be doing well so far. Of course, she was sure that if he had any romantic interests or crushes, she'd be the last person he'd come to. She was, after all, his sister. No doubt he'd be embarrassed as hell.

"Ok, get your backpack and let's go."

Obediently, Xaviar swung his book-heavy bag over his shoulders before following his sister out into the chill winter air. It had snowed overnight, and there were several inches of fresh powder that hadn't yet been soiled by the plough that ran the city streets. At times like this, Cece could find their run-down neighborhood beautiful, and pretend that they were just a normal family enjoying the holidays.

She drove Xaviar to school. She had refused to let him ride the bus ever since he told her one of his classmates had bought a gun on board. It was gas money spent but, if her brother got to school safely, it was a sacrifice she was willing to make.

"Did you do your English homework?" She quizzed him, her eyes on the snow-slick rode as she headed toward the High School.

Xaviar nodded, his expression long suffering. "And math, and science. You only checked on me five times last night."

"I check on you because I like to see you using that noggin of yours for something besides video games and drawing."

"Suuuure. You live to torture me." Xaviar's light tone let her know he didn't mean it in the slightest.

"I live to see you succeed. If that means torturing you, then I will put you on the rack and crank it up to the nth degree."

"Harsh, Cece." He grinned at her as she pulled up in front of a huge brick building marked with its customary New York number. As she put the car in park, she frowned slightly, watching gangs of children huddled about the front entryway, doing God knew what. She didn't even want to contemplate her brother joining their ranks.

Leaning over, she placed her hand on Xaviar's arm, a small smile creeping back onto her face at his exasperated expression. "Have a good day, OK?"

"Same as the last one, but I'll try." He returned the gesture before making a face as she pecked his cheek warmly.

"Love you."

"You too." He slipped of the car, embarrassed, as he pulled up his hood and began jogging for the front entry of the school. After he'd disappeared, Cece merely leaned against the steering wheel, taking a deep breath. This couldn't fly for much longer. Xaviar needed to be educated in a more stable environment.

But where the hell was she going to find the money for such a thing?

**

Alexander woke to his intercom buzzing.

It wasn't the first, nor would it be the last time he'd slept in his office. The sleek leather sofa in the anteroom was, in fact, a sofa bed, and he utilized it regularly. He'd been up the previous night until almost three in the morning going over documents for a prominent case and now, it was almost eight.

No surprise that Melody, his personal assistant, had chosen to give him a wake up call. He had to be in the courtroom in an hour. With a low, tired groan, he forced himself upright, running fingers through dark blonde hair. He'd run on less sleep than he had now before, and done so efficiently. All he needed was a few cups of Colombian roast.

He rose to his feet, stretching his well muscled form in a lingering motion. When his intercom buzzed again, he slipped from the anteroom and into his office proper, pressing the button to answer. "Melody. I'll be dressed and ready to head to the courthouse in thirty minutes. Call Spelling and make sure that he shows up *on time*."

"...um, Mr. Cross?"

He froze.

The voice answering him on the intercom was most definitely not the calm, calculated tones of his long-time personal assistant, Melody. Instead, it sounded distinctly like that of the paralegal who often brought him his coffee in the morning. Brown eyes, dark hair...Margaret something or other.

"Margaret?" His voice was firm and authoritative as he questioned the young woman on the other side of the com. "Where is Melody?"

The woman's nervousness was apparent in the way her voice trembled over the reply. "Well, Sir...she left suddenly yesterday evening. Simply...resigned and walked out. Cited some familial issues or something of that sort."

Alexander cursed under his breath.

Melody had been with him for the past two years. The middle-aged woman had been concise, punctual, and had worked magic when it came to tracking down difficult clients and figures. If she had just walked out on him, the matter must have been something very serious indeed. She knew he didn't take such things lightly.

Part of him wondered what emergency had torn the best P.A he'd had from his clutches on the morning of a major trial, but he knew the more pressing matter would be finding someone to fill her shoes. His office normally ran like a well oiled machine with her at the helm, and now, he would have to work overtime to ensure that things remained that way.

Raising a hand to his temple, he rubbed at the ache beginning between his eyes.

This day was going to be hellish.

"Margaret, are you still there?"

"Y-yes, Mr. Cross." The girl had always been flustered by him, and it appeared that she hadn't lost any of her jitters, even when they weren't in the same room.

"I need you to call Jared Spelling and make sure he makes it to this morning's trial on time. You should find his number in Melody's contact book. If he does not answer," the man was infamous for flaking when it came to matters concerning his public image, "then you will drive to his house and retrieve him. Is that understood?"

"Of course, Mr. Cross." She seemed to know not to ask him where to find the address. She had merely to look through Melody's plethora of resources and she'd discover it soon enough. He'd been working with Spelling for the past six months. The man's information should be plastered all over their most recent files.

He left his office, heading for the small stash of clothing he kept in the room that adjoined it. As he extracted an immaculately pressed blue shirt and slacks from a small wardrobe, his brilliant mind worked overtime. As long as the trial today went off without a hitch, he should have ample time to find a new PA. As much as he hated to admit it, he'd be dependent upon Margaret's efficiency for the morning.

He frowned.

He shouldn't be too hard on the girl, he knew. She was a twenty something working on her own law degree to become an attorney. Alexander simply didn't have time for incompetence – not at this juncture. He'd gotten to where he was by both requiring and providing excellence.

As well as his drive and commitment to justice.

His eyes darkened as he remembered the tragic events of his youth that had driven him to seek out a career in law. As much as he hated to dwell on the past, these were memories he couldn't afford to ignore. He used them to galvanize his efforts if ever he felt the frustration and stress of his job overwhelming him.

All he had to do was remember the blood spatter, his father's infuriated screams and the endless, torturous trials that had ruled his twenty second year. The pain was more than enough to rejuvenate him, and it was that inspiration that would get him through today.

He slipped into his slacks, fastening them low on his waist before shrugging into his shirt. As he did up the ivory buttons, he stared at his image in the mirror. A blonde haired behemoth of a man stared back at him, green eyes intelligent and alert despite lack of sleep, dark blonde hair mussed and yet untended to. There was half a day's growth of stubble that he'd have to take care of, but once he had, he would be instantly recognizable.

Manhattan district attorney Alexander Cross.

At thirty eight, he was the youngest man in the city's history to hold the title, but damn if he hadn't worked for it. After his mother's death, he had worked with almost animalistic fervor in his studies. Overnight, he changed his major from engineering to pre-law and flew through the four year curriculum in less than two. He'd conquered law school with much the same intensity in just under two and a half years and his high scores on the bar saw firms clamoring to offer him his first position.

Becoming an attorney, however, had only been the beginning of his ambitions. He'd risen quickly through the ranks at Pearson and Pearson, taking on the most difficult cases and the most impossible clients. The only clients he refused were those who were very obviously on the wrong side of the law. He was...disinclined to help criminals try and escape their due punishment.

He'd seen enough of that in his lifetime.

His reputation for hard work and dedication to his morals had earned him a pristine reputation. Within two years he'd made partner in his firm and in another two, they were lending him out for state cases. When elections had come up for the empty District Attorney seat six years ago, he'd run but been outpaced by Derek Hallowell, a legendary law shark twice his age. The man had failed, however, to up the city's conviction rate of hardened criminals, and so when he'd stepped down, Alexander had been an obvious choice.

The first term had been more difficult than he'd ever imagined. The crusade he'd endeavored upon had tested the limits of his endurance and his sanity. Long hours, corrupt authorities, and uncooperative clients had been only a few of the roadblocks he'd faced. He'd had to answer for the mayor and the police chief every time he'd made a mistake and several times, he'd questioned the path he'd taken.

The second term had come easier. He'd grown firmer in his convictions, learned exactly how to root out corruption, and whose elbows to rub which way to achieve his goals.

In the courtroom, he had a reputation as a ruthless prosecutor and a relentless interrogator. Outside, he was the face of justice – one criminals both respected and feared. Who he really was, however, Alexander feared had been lost in the last few years. All that was left were the cases – cases and convictions.

One less criminal on the street. One less kilo of drugs in neighborhoods that desperately needed clean slates.

Thus, finding a new PA was of tantamount importance. Without one, his office would falter; and if it faltered, he faltered.

With a bit of luck, Margaret would find Spelling. The man had been caught the previous year taking money for information on crooked cops. Though his cause was noble, his methods weren't – which was where Alexander came in. He needed to ensure the man didn't serve jail time for his attempts to clean up their city, and also to convince him to stop treating such serious matters like cash cows.

Spelling was a good man deep down; just spectacularly lazy and covetous.

Alexander knotted his tie expertly before slipping it over his head and settling about his neck. He moved to the private restroom in his office for a quick shave before slicking his hair back and adding a hint of aftershave. The sting served to wake him almost as well as a cup of coffee and, as it did, he gave himself a last once over in the mirror.

He could not afford for today to go wrong. Spelling would serve a good asset in the future.

He stepped back into his office, checking over the few messages Melody had left before her departure before slipping into his suit jacket and searching for his leather overcoat. Not a moment after he'd picked it up, his phone buzzed from the front pocket.

He checked his watch.

Forty minutes before he had to be at the courthouse.

When he read the caller ID, he frowned, before answering. "This is Cross."

"Not even a proper greeting for your old dad these days, Alex?"

The D.A sighed, hoping that his burgeoning headache wasn't going to grow to massive proportions. "I have a lot of work, Dad. You know I'll be home for the holidays, as always." Since his mother's death, his father had grown rather dependent on him. The old man had followed his harrowing rise to notoriety with skeptical eyes, but as soon as his position was cemented, he had pushed him to prosecute every criminal he could to the furthest extent of the law – or even beyond it.

The skepticism, Alexander could forgive. His father had been hurting, the loss of his wife a devastating blow. However, him to suggest that he knew how to do his son's job was another matter entirely. He could not go about smashing windshields, burning tires, or beating men within inches of their lives.

Though there were rapists, murderers and drug kingpins galore in the city, his job necessitated that he work within the parameters of the law. Venturing outside it would put everything he had worked for at risk.

"I know your job is important to you, son. Being the DA is no walk in the park. It might help if you hired some people to help you out with the more unsavory-"

"Dad." Alexander cut him off before he could say anything that might result in his own incarceration. "I have to be at the courthouse in thirty. Do you need something?"

Edward Cross' tone sobered, as it always did when he was thwarted. "I was actually just calling to see if you contacted the Munster girl."

"Who?" Alexander was packing all the paperwork he

needed for the trial into his briefcase. The name his father mentioned hurtled over his head and way into left field, where it remained, unattended to.

"Felicia Munster?" His father's tone was dry as he repeated the question. "Tall, curvy redhead? Amazing eyes? PhD in astrophysics at MIT? I worked a few months to get that dinner set up. Do you even remember the woman at all?"

Alexander suppressed a groan. His father had set him up on a number of dates with Manhatttan's intellectual and monetary elite in the past year. Good-looking girls from prestigious families, none of whom could even begin to fathom the issues he faced everyday. It wasn't as if he didn't appreciate his old man's efforts. At the very least, they'd gotten him laid a few times, and that was always a good stress reliever; but if he was trying to find a match of the "having and holding forever" caliber, than Alexander wasn't interested.

His work was his wife, mistress and lover all in one. Until he decided he'd made enough of a difference in the system – that criminals like the ones who'd gotten away with murdering his mother would never see such lenience again - he would work fifty hour weeks and wake up with night sweats. It was an impossible task, he knew, but one that he faced with gusto.

After all, his methods were working.

"Adeline Munster." He remembered her. All she'd wanted to talk about was how smart she was. Granted, the woman was brilliant, but the way she'd bragged her way through the evening hadn't been attractive. "No. I haven't called her. Don't plan to."

"Damn it, Alex. I'm trying to set you up with someone who can take some of this stress off your shoulders." He left his office quietly after making the bed, heading down the quiet hall towards the elevator bay as his father chastised him. "You can't tackle the entire city alone."

"And I'm sure some manicured, coiffed socialite would love to be right there by my side. Look, Dad, I see your point but I don't have much room in my life for a woman right now. Everything comes secondary to the job."

A frustrated sound emitted from his father's side of the line. "I wish your mother were here. You'd listen to her."

Alexander's heart twisted painfully in his chest. "She's not here. She's gone because some crackhead downed her in her prime. Should I be out attending social functions or making sure that no other families are ever disappointed the way we were?"

Silence.

He'd spoken too harshly, perhaps, but it was imperative that his father understood. His battles weren't fought with fists or in rings, but with words and convictions. Though he had all the strength and frustration to battle criminals in an all out brawl, taking their freedom from them was both cleaner and more devastating.

A woman would never understand that.

"Dad, I have to go. Look, we'll talk about it at Christmas, Ok?" The cold air hit him like a brick wall and Alexander pulled his scarf up over his mouth as he strode through the parking garage to his gleaming black Mercedes.

"Sure, son. Sure."

The line went dead and he sighed, tossing the phone down in the passenger seat as he started the car.

It was going to be a long day.

**

"Girl, you look like you haven't gotten any decent sleep in weeks."

Cece's head jerked up from where she'd been lost in her own thoughts. Xaviar had a school trip to the Pokonoes coming up in two weeks and she was wondering where she was going to get the money to send him. She was two months behind on the rent and her car needed new tires, badly.

Jasmine, one of her best friends, was peering at her as they stood in line at a posh coffee house on the upper west side of Manhattan. The slightly older woman had suggested that they meet for hot drinks and catch up, as Cece hadn't been able to make it out in ages. It was supposed to be a fun outing, but instead, she just found herself dwelling on her issues.

"I'm...I'm ok." The truth was, she'd had more than her fair share of sleepless nights in the past week. Her apartment was freezing, and there were days when she had to choose between gas or dinner. As it was, her stomach was growling. She'd skipped breakfast to make sure Xaviar could have a full plate of eggs and bacon. He needed it more than she did.

"If there is something you are not, honey, it's OK."

Jasmine was the picture of young success. At the tender age of thirty two she was marketing manager of accounts for the conglomerate that owned Gap, Banana Republic, and Old Navy. She had an amazing head for figures and dogged ambition that had rocketed her to the top of her field, and she was living the dream. There had been a time when Cece thought she might have reached her girlfriend's level, now, she couldn't help but feel a twinge of envy. Jasmine had not been laid off during the economic cut-backs. She was instrumental in the running of her company.

Just as Cece had thought she herself had been.

"I'm just a little stressed right now." The coffee house was packed, and the line snaked toward the register slowly as she spoke to her friend. "You know, job hunting is awful these days. I can't find anything in my field and money just gets tighter and tighter." She frowned, running a hand through the tangled mess of her dark curls.

"A little stressed?" Jasmine gray gaze was skeptical as she gazed at her friend. "Anyone going through what you're going through would be at their wits end, Cecilia." She seemed to consider before she continued. "You know, if you needed, I could lend you something to help you out-"

"*No.*" The younger woman cut her off almost sharply before her expression softened and she shook her head. "I mean, sorry, Jas, but you know I can't take anything. I'll figure something out. I always do."

They finally reached the front of the line and Cece

contemplated the menu. Though she had expected high Manhattan prices, she was dismayed to find that the only thing within her five dollar budget was a plain latte. With a sigh, she made to order it – only to be cut off by her companion beside her.

"I'm buying." Jasmine's expression was firm, and stayed that way even when Cece opened her mouth to protest. "Girl, don't even. You won't let me lend you anything so I'm damn well going to treat you to coffee and cake. You look like you could use some." She poked her friend's growling stomach with a small smile.

For once, Cece was too hungry to argue much. When she attempted to indicate the latte to the amused cashier, Jasmine just rolled her eyes and ordered them both thick slices of black forest cake and decadent Chestnut Macchiatos. She pushed away the money Cece offered before whisking her to a nearby table that had just been vacated.

As they made themselves comfortable, Jasmine fixed her with an intense stare. "Cece, this has to stop. I know you're trying to be noble and take care of Xaviar on your own, but when you need help, you need help. I'm not going to think any less of you."

Cece merely shook her head firmly. "I'm not worried about that. And I'm not saying your offer's not generous, because it is. You know I don't mean any offense, Jas, I just can't depend on people. The one person I ever depended on..." She trailed off, her gaze growing distant as she remembered years of abuse with her father.

"Cece, your father was an asshole." Jasmine's voice was flat, "He did you wrong. Real wrong. But he's not exactly a shining example of the charity in the world."

Cece snorted. That was the understatement of the century. "I know."

Their coffee and dessert arrived and for a moment, neither of them said anything. With the cake in front of her, there was little Cecilia could do but tuck in hungrily as Jasmine watched with an empathetic expression. Cece was done with her cake long before Jasmine even started, and was sipping at the creamy

Righting Wrongs

sweetness of her chestnut macchiato when her friend next spoke.

"How about a job?"

At that, her ears perked up. Cece raised her head to fix her friend with inquiring honey colored eyes. "What do you mean, 'a job'?"

A slow smile spread across Jasmine's gorgeous face and Cece repressed a groan. She'd been had. The woman knew exactly how to pique her interest.

"You don't want a loan, so how about I give you an in on a job?"

Her tone was carefully optimistic – enough so that Cece could guess what was coming next. "What kind of job?"

"Well..." Jasmine took a sip of a drink and then a bite of her cake, chewing thoughtfully. "It's not in your field, but the money would be good. And you'd get to work in Manhattan."

Cece's heart sank slightly. Fashion was and always would be her passion. It had been far to much for her to expect that Jasmine would happen to know of an empty position in the cutthroat fashion industry. However, she wasn't idiotic enough to look a gift horse in the mouth. If there was well-paying work to be had, she might as well investigate.

"Alright, so, spill. What kind of position is it?"

Her companion grinned, showing straight, even white teeth in contrast to her dark skin. "I have a contact in the district attorney's office, and she's brought it to my attention that the man is looking for a new PA. Open interviews."

Cece groaned as she took another sip of her drink. A PA? She'd never get through the door. She didn't have the background for it. "Wait, wait, *listen*." Jasmine interrupted her pouting before she could get too far. "There's supposedly a need for more organizational orientation than actual experience. According to Carol, my contact, the DA is a sticker for work delivered on time and a penchant for working around the unworkable. That, my dear, is the story of your life."

It was true. When she'd first started in the fashion industry, she'd been given the most difficult projects. Trial by fire – and she'd surmounted every challenge presented to her. It had made the loss of the job all the more devastating.

"Sounds...promising." She had to give Jasmine that. A high-ranking PA position with little to no experience required? She could type – and at quite a rapid clip too. Whatever else the DA required, she was sure she was up to the challenge. It might even distract her from the troubles she had at home.

Troubles that, in and of themselves, would be alleviated after a few months of steady work.

"It is. I could recommend you for the job. It would mean you'd be first in line to interview." Jasmine took a leisurely bite of her cake. "And I think that would be the end of the story."

Cece allowed herself a small smile. "Your confidence in me is breathtaking."

Jasmine laughed. "I know you. You'll get it."

"What about him?" Her companion voiced the inquiry, her brow knit together in inquiry. "The D.A. Alexander Cross, right? I've heard of him."

"Who hasn't?" Jasmine's eyes immediately brightened as her cheeks flushed with color. "He's got a vendetta against anyone with a serious criminal background and a personal mission to clean up the streets. That would be nothing new if the man weren't succeeding! Cece, he's got an ninety percent conviction rate. *Ninety percent*. It's incredible."

Hm. Cece had heard something about the man being the new head of justice in the city, but Jasmine was making him sound like some sort of avenging angel. "Not to mention," the elder woman continued, "He's fucking gorgeous."

That drew a laugh from Cece. "Oh, Christ, Jasmine. Only you."

"Not *only* me!" Her friend protested in mock outrage. "Honey, the man is fine white chocolate just begging to be tasted. Have you *seen* him?"

The most Cece could recall were fuzzy images from cases on TV and a few posters from elections years ago. Nothing concrete. "You know what, let me hush. You can see for yourself when you interview with the man." Jasmine pulled out her blackberry, her fingers racing over the keys dexterously. "What time is good for you?"

This was all moving pretty fast. Not that she was complaining – a job would mean a world of difference for both her and Xaviar. Jasmine might as well have been offering her pure gold.

"Um...anytime between nine and three, really. I have to get Xaviar from school in the evenings."

Jasmine chewed her lower lip pensively as her eyes scanned her blackberry. For a moment, she didn't speak, merely answering messages as they arrived with soft *dings*. After two minutes, her head lifted and she cast a brilliant smile upon Cece. "Ok. You're in. Ten in the morning tomorrow."

"Tomorrow?" Cece almost choked on her coffee. "Where is this, exactly?"

"D.A's office downtown." Jasmine's tone was almost gleeful as she downed the last of her drink in a large gulp. "I'll text you the address. You are about to be employed with the most sinful hunk of man flesh in the city."

In reply, Cece merely rolled her eyes. She sincerely doubted the man would live up to Jasmine's claims; and besides, even if he did, she highly doubted such high profile Caucasian man would see her as anything more than his hired help. That thought, however, wasn't enough to quell the rising hope in her gut.

This was an oppurtunity for a new start; and if there was even the slightest chance that she could get that job, she was going for it.

CHAPTER 2 - CHANGES

The next morning dawned with frosty sunlight and, for once, it seemed that everything was going Cece's way. Xaviar got up on time for school and chose to grab a breakfast sandwich on the way with his own money, leaving her free to gobble up the few eggs they had left. After breakfast, she dressed carefully in her most conservative business attire after washing and brushing her hair carefully into a neat chignon atop her head. For appearances sake she applied just the slightest bit of makeup and broke out the coat she used only for special occasions. She'd long since sold her others to pay rent.

After preparing for nearly an hour, she gave herself a critical one over in the cracked bathroom mirror.

Cece supposed she was lucky. Though she was nearing her thirty-first birthday, wrinkles had yet to show on her smooth, caramel colored skin. Her honey eyes were large and bright, despite having slept poorly the previous night, and were outlined with just a hint of mascara. Her usually wild curls had been tamed and she'd wrestled her curves into a white button up and a navy high-low skirt she'd often worn to business meetings when she'd worked in the fashion industry. Thankfully, the outfit lent a conservative air to her ample bosom and wide hips. With her glossy black heels and slightly rouged lips, she'd say she looked fit to be personal assistant to a district attorney.

She could only hope that he felt the same way.

She shrugged into her coat, shivering as her breath frosted on the chill air and she hurried downstairs.

It was only when she was in her car, in the Holland Tunnel, when the butterflies began to set in. They continued all the way downtown, where she paid for a fifteen dollar parking ticket she couldn't really afford in the upscale lower west side.

The district attorney. She was about to meet the district

attorney for the entire city.

It was no small feat, she measured. If Jasmine hadn't used her contacts, she doubted she would ever have been seen for an interview, let alone considered for the job. If she got it, she would definitely have to take her girlfriend out on a thank-you dinner.

The D.A's office was at the top of a massive building that housed three other law firms. After announcing her appointment at the front desk Cece was signed in and directed to one of three elevator bays. On the ride up, her butterflies only grew more intense.

On the thirtieth floor, she stepped out into an atmosphere of silence and muted colors. There were several dark wood cubicles, in each of which an attorney worked tirelessly rounding up information for a number of cases. The walls and carpets were a dark maroon color, with even darker furniture adorning the waiting area. The overall effect served both imposing and zen simultaneously.

There was no one at the secretary's desk, and Cece was loathe to break the silence in which the lawyers worked. And so, silently, she moved to take a seat in one of the armchairs in the sitting area, prepared to wait.

No sooner had she sat down, however, then a door at the far end of the office opened and a very tall, very skinny brunette appeared, her expression as nervous as that of a skittish colt. She made a beeline for Cece, relief stark on her face as soon as their eyes met. "You're Cecilia Thompson?"
She held out a hand to shake and, as Cece did so, she noticed that the girl's palm was cold and clammy.

Something was very clearly stressing her out. "Yes. You can call me Cece."

"Margaret. This way, please, Cecilia." It was like the young woman hadn't even heard her. She was lost in her own world. "Mr. Cross is expecting you." She uttered the man's name with a kind of reverence and fear that made it clear that he was the source of her nerves.

Cece's own butterflies whipped up into a frenzy as the

young woman led her through the cubicles and to the opposite end of the office where a tall door emblazoned with the name *Alexander Cross* stood out in vivid detail. "He'll be in his office – through the anteroom. I wouldn't make him wait."

With that, she scurried off back to her desk, quite clearly glad to be as far from Cross' personal office as humanly possible.

With her own sweaty palm, Cece slowly reached out to open the door in front of her.

The room beyond was decorated in much the same way as the main office. Muted pine colors adorned the walls, as well as furniture that smelled of leather and tobacco, cleaned to a gleaming finish. Taking a deep breath, Cece let herself inside, closing the door behind her before she crossed the span of it – bigger than both her and Xaviar's bedrooms combined.

She paused just outside the door to the office proper, steeling herself. She was about to meet Jasmine's angel of justice.

But what kind of angel terrified a poor young girl?

"Come." The deep, commanding baritone from the other side of the door made her jump a moment before she pushed the door open in acquiescence.

Cross' office was the same soft pine color as his anteroom, the walls lined with innumerable bookcases filled with reading materials. A window shed light on the pinewood floor, upon which two armchairs rested facing a rosewood desk. The desk, Cece noticed immediately, had been custom made for someone very tall – and the moment her gaze fell on Alexander Cross, she knew why.

Her breath was stolen from her.

The man was massive. Broad shoulders stretched taut a crisply tailored green button up. Startlingly muscled arms contracted as writing was scribbled over several documents, creasing the sleeves of the garment. Cece didn't think she'd ever seen a man so large – especially not one in a suit. Though she herself was a good six one in heels, this man would be certain to dwarf her if and when he stood. Long legs were crossed beneath his desk in trim black slacks and well polished shoes.

Righting Wrongs

At her entry, the man lifted his head and Cece was assaulted with an emotion she thought she'd forgotten how to feel.
Pure, liquid lust slammed through her.
Dark blonde hair was slicked back from Cross' high forehead, revealing piercing, impassive green eyes set in an angular, masculine face. The line of his jaw appeared carved from marble and shaved absolutely smooth, his nose high and aquiline. An unexpectedly full mouth softened the overall appearance without detracting from it's stunning, visceral beauty; and no sooner had her eyes fallen on it than Cece was assaulted by thoughts of what that mouth would feel like running over ever inch of her skin leisurely as that deep, silky baritone whispered ungodly things against her flesh.
The images made her cheeks color and, though she knew the man couldn't read minds, she found herself suddenly unable to meet Cross' emerald gaze.
She was in a world of trouble.

**

Alexander had started his interviews as soon as he was able. Though Margeret had some trouble bringing Spelling down to the courthouse, he'd been there on time and the trial had gone off without a hitch. Instead of five years in jail, the man had gotten sixty days of community service; and Alexander made sure that his days of extorting money for snitching were over.
The man would be on his payroll as soon as he finished his service. He could protect him better that way and God knew the information he provided would be invaluable.
A week later, he had begun to consider Melody's replacement. The idea of employing Margaret was, of course, ridiculous. The girl jumped every time he spoke and was often too flustered to follow his commands with any sense of efficiency. She took it personally, he knew, when he became frustrated with her, and he could not afford to work with such a thin-skinned individual. Melody had been heartier. When he bellowed and

blustered, she had bowed with the wind and taken his tirades like a champ.

And so, of course, when Carol Mathers, a fellow attorney, had called with a personal recommendation, he'd jumped at the chance. According to her, although the applicant had no prior experience working as a PA, she had excellent people skills and was used to overcoming obstacles. The last quality, for Alexander, was crucial. His P.A was like an extension of himself and he did not give in when faced with a challenging case or client.

Even after all Carol had told him, however, he hadn't expected the woman who'd walked through his office door.

Cecelia Thompson had the face of an angel and a body as sinful as a succubus. Despite the fact that she'd obviously tried to dress appropriately for the interview, not even the shirt she wore – buttoned to the throat – could disguise the generous curve of her breasts. Nor could the skirt she'd paired with it mask ample hips that curved out from a tiny waist. Her legs were long, as was her neck, and though he couldn't say he'd had a history of being drawn to ethnic women, her smooth, toffee-hued skin tempted him to kiss and lick – to see if she tasted as soft as she looked.

Almond shaped eyes the color of honey took him in as he did her, set above a pert, small nose and audaciously full lips. He had to swallow thickly against the urge to cross the room and jerk her into his arms – to drink from that ungodly beautiful mouth.

Dark curls had been tamed into a bun atop her head, but that could be easily resolved. He could run his fingers through the soft locks, releasing the pins and bands until her curls tumbled free over her shoulders. Then, he could carry her into his anteroom and ravish the hell out of her.

Christ.

He couldn't remember the last time a woman had inspired such dark thoughts in him. For him, laying women was a means to an end – a distraction that tamed lusts that would otherwise distract him from his work. But this woman...she would have to be loved slowly. He would taste every inch of her skin and have her begging for him by the time he slipped inside her...

As if she could read his thoughts, her face colored slightly and she dropped her gaze, clearing her throat uncomfortably.

The gesture snapped him from his carnal thoughts.

This would not do. It would not do at all. It would be damn near impossible for him to work with this woman around him for any protracted length of time.

However, sending her from his office without even questioning her...it would be an insult to Carol – and another day he'd have to spend with Margaret.

Forcibly clearing the lustful haze from his thoughts, Alexander finally spoke. "Please, take a seat, Mrs. Thompson."

"Miss." Her gaze rose to meet his for a fraction of a second and those honey eyes almost undid him. Then, she looked away, moving towards one of the armchairs before him. "Just Miss."

Unmarried. Interesting.

"*Miss* Thompson." As she took a seat, crossing her legs primly, he bit back the desire to inch her skirt up over her thighs and feel the downy skin he knew he would find there. "Thank you for coming. You came very highly recommended by Carol. I'm sure she's told you about the position I need to fill, but let me go over some of the finer aspects the job would entail."

She didn't interrupt him, her eyes now gazing at him with rapt attention. "A P.A in my employ is not only a P.A. They are a secretary, a paralegal of sorts, a little black book of information on clients I might find difficult to locate. They keep my affairs in order as well as understanding that I have no tolerance for repeated failure, tardiness or complaints. When you are in this office, I will need you to help me wage war on this city's dirty underbelly. How does this strike you?"

When he had interviewed Melody, years earlier, the older woman had chosen her answer very carefully.

Cecilia Thompson didn't miss a beat.

"It strikes me as a lot of work for a P.A" Her voice was rich and low, like dark honey flowing from a spoon. "You're asking for long hours and steadfast commitment to your cause, which might be difficult for some people." Her eyes were clear and her speech articulate in her answer.

He was intrigued.

"But not for you?"

"Mr. Cross," Her tone was patient, polite, and very succinct, "I have an eye for detail, and I love a challenge. Additionally, when I contemplate the things you seek to accomplish for this city, I think that it would be criminal of me *not* to help you the best of my ability."

"And how is that ability, would you say?" When he leaned forward, he could smell her. Cherries, vanilla, and something spicier.

Something exotic.

"Impeccable. I don't give up. I don't quit."

"And if I ask you to drag clients to courthouses when they're no shows? Or to run important case files to other attorneys in the wee small hours of the morning?"

"Those requests are requests you make of me because you need me. My job would be to see that those needs are met to ensure that your office runs smoothly."

A diplomatic answer, to say the least. Inexplicably, Alexander found himself rising from his chair. Almost everyone he knew, upon first encounter with him, had been cowed by his almost seven foot height. It was a tool that he used to his advantage both in the courtroom and outside of it, and he used it well.

If Cecilia was intimidated by his stature, it didn't show on her face.

He rounded his desk to stand next to her chair and her scent enveloped him. He bit back a groan as he raised his hand to the back of the armchair, just brushing the soft skin at the nape of her neck. He felt, rather than saw the shiver that traveled down her spine, and it took a moment for her to look up and meet his gaze.

"If I need you, you will be there. These are your words, correct?"

She moistened her lips – a brief darting of her tongue

across her plump red mouth that threatened his sanity. "Exactly my words."

He needed to back off. Being this close to her was dangerous. The tension in the air was electric and the woman would have to be a fool not to sense it.

This woman was no fool. She *was* gorgeous beyond reason, and her tongue was quick, her mind even more so. If she was as aggressive in her work as she had been through his questioning, she could be a valuable asset to him.

But if he kept her here, he could risk losing his head over her.

The decision was a hard one. In the end, he chose a question to help him decide.

"Cecilia, if you were to make one change in this office, what would it be?" Her eyes widened in surprise before quickly becoming pensive. Though he thought she might consider for a few minutes, barely thirty seconds had passed before she spoke.

"A suggestion, I think, less than a real change."

He arched a brow, intrigued. "Tell me."

Here, she hesitated a moment – just a moment – before continuing on. "That girl...outside. Margaret. She's terrified of you, but she also worships you. I'd find a good balance. Fear doesn't do well for morale."

Color him surprised. Melody, he believed, had rattled something off about scheduling and cutting break times to increase efficiency. This woman had noticed Margaret's proclivity to fall to pieces when he was around and was suggesting that he...be nicer to her? A single paralegal in his office?

"Ms. Thompson, I run this office the way I do because it works. If I make Margaret nervous, it is because she overreacts to my presence."

"Or because you're a seven foot tall ruthless D.A who runs the city *and* her life."

For a moment, he was at an actual loss for words. It had been years since someone other than an opponent had so blatantly questioned the way he ran things. When he spoke again, his voice was low and dangerous.

"Are you usually so straightforward?"

Though she swallowed, her fingers tightening on the arms of the chair, her steady gaze did not waver.

"Always."

Heat flared through him.

Straightening, Alexander forced himself to walk away, lest he do something he'd regret. Slowly, he settled himself behind his desk once more, taking up his pen as he extracted a new document from his top drawer.

A W-9.

"We'll start on a temporary basis." At his words, Cecilia's face was immediately flooded by a bliss the likes of which he hadn't seen in a long while. Her lips turned up in a breathtaking smile as her eyes widened and she inhaled sharply. He wasn't sure, but he thought he might have seen moisture glimmering at the corners of her eyes.

As quickly as the expression had appeared, however, it was gone, and her cool calm was back in place.

Even so, it was too late. Her smile had twisted something deep in Alexander's gut and made him feel the distinctive discomfort of wondering what had made her smile like he was her port in a storm. He forced himself to fill out the W-9, handing it to her when it was complete. "Take this to Margaret and she'll get you settled with the additional paperwork."

Cecilia leapt to her feet, the form in hand. "Thank you, Mr. Cross. You won't regret this decision."

His lips quirked slightly at her confidence. "Be sure that I don't." With that she turned on her heel and hurried from his office, leaving a trail of cherry-vanilla scent in her wake. The moment she disappeared, Alex let his pen fall to his desk, the enticing swaying of her hips emblazoned upon his mind.

He had just hired her. He longed to strip the clothes from her body at first sight and now she was to work at his side five days a weak.

What kind of masochist had he become?

**

Cece had been confident at her interview. To be honest, she'd been so confident that she'd shocked even herself. Inside, her body had been reeling with the closeness of Alexander Cross, his low tones sending thrums of arousal through her every time he spoke.

He challenged her.

Forced her to think on her feet.

And honestly, by the time he'd stood over her, Cece had begun to think working for him might not be the best idea. The man smelled fresh and spicy, and the warmth of him almost made her swoon. He had power, and he knew it. His final question had just been to test exactly how audacious her answer could be – how much she thought she could get away with.

It hadn't been much, really. But it had been enough.

Cece had no doubt that poor Margaret would probably suffer until Cross burned her out and she fled to greener pastures, but at least she'd spoken up for the girl – and, she was sure, challenged Cross' perspective of her in the process.

The suggestion had gotten her hired, hadn't it?

How, exactly, she maintained the position remained to be seen. And even though she was ecstatic as she left the office, Cece knew that keeping her cool on a day to day basis would be no easy task.

Being around Cross was intoxicating. Though she knew that she should probably find his commanding manner irritating or, as Margaret did, downright frightening, she couldn't help but feel the titillation his commands offered her long neglected sex drive. The man didn't ask, he ordered. He didn't request, he demanded.

She couldn't help but wonder, would he be so dominating in the bedroom?

The thought made her frown as she bent over the stove,

working on Xaviar's dinner in her African muumuu. She was sure the man had an all plethora of monied New York socialites to satisfy whatever carnal desires he had. She was only going to get herself into trouble imagining what that amazing body would look like stripped down, muscles bulging as his fingers sought out her most secret havens...

"Sis!"

The front door slammed, jerking her from her naughty thoughts. Her face flushed, Cece quickly glanced over her shoulder with a small, guilty smile. "Hey! How was school?"

"Boring, as usual. There was a knife fight in chemistry though."

As the boy settled at the table, letting his backpack slide to the ground, Cece's frown returned. A knife fight? In a chemistry lab? "Why the hell would they bring knives into a science lab?"

Xaviar grinned in amusement at her profanity. "Language, Cece."

Caught, she merely shook her head, disturbed by news of this latest violence. "*You* don't say those words. You know they're bad. Now, what happened in the fight?"

"One of the boys got slashed up pretty bad. They took him out on a stretcher. The rest of us had to attend an assembly where we promised to report any threatening activity." The teenager had a rather blasé look on his face for having been witness to something so gruesome. "Dunno how much that's going to help though."

Cece turned off the greens on the stove, turning to face her brother with a concerned expression. "Xaviar, promise me you won't ever do anything that stupid."

"Are you kidding me?" The boy's eyes went wide. "What I want to bring a knife to school for? I'd rather get beat up than go to jail!"

Thank God for that. Silently, Cece wrapped her arms tightly around the teen, grateful that he seemed to have the sense their father had so lacked. "Good. That's good."

Xaviar squirmed from her grip, his face red as he changed

Righting Wrongs

the subject. "Yeah, yeah..." He spoke gruffly, his eyes averted. "What's for dinner?"

As the question, Cece sighed. She hadn't started work yet, and as such, their food supply was still pretty low. "Some chicken...from yesterday. I got some good greens today though." Most of them would go to Xaviar. He always came home ravenous. She made him a plate and he dug in. She was grateful, she reflected, that the teenager wasn't of the nasty breed who might complain or scorn the food she provided. He always tucked in with gusto, and now, finally, she'd be on her way to getting him back to the food he needed.

"Hey, guess what." She smiled as she picked at her collards. Xaviar's head jerked up from where he tore at a chicken leg, his mouth half full.

"What?"

Cece suppressed a smile. "I got a job today."

Her brother's eyes widened. "A fashion job, like your old one?" Though he, like every typical male, disdained the fashion world, Xaviar did like to draw; and so, he could appreciate the intricate designs his sister fabricated for her projects.

"Well...no." Cece was a bit embarrassed to admit this tidbit, as she constantly affirmed to her brother that he could be anything he wanted if he tried. "But it's in the D.A's office. I'll get to work in the city again."

"That sounds...ok." The teen picked up his second piece of chicken. "Does this mean we get to go back to Harlem?"

His question made Cece's smile falter slightly. She couldn't promise anything so drastic so soon. They were so deep in the hole with her old student loans, rent, and bills, it would take a while for her to work her way back onto solid ground. The moment she did, however, she would put all her strength into getting them out of south Brooklyn and getting Xaviar into a better school.

"Well, not now, but maybe in a year or so. How does that sound? We'll move back to Harlem and you can go to the gifted school again."

"Sounds good." Xaviar's grunt was low, his eyes distant, and Cece lamented that they couldn't make the change for him sooner. The boy had been living in awful conditions for long enough that she was sure he wondered if they'd ever have their old life back.

They would, if she had anything to do with it.

They *had* to.

After dinner, she sent Xaviar upstairs to do his homework and washed the dishes, making a face at all the little flies in the sink. They might not be able to move out soon, but she was definitely going to spend more money on bug bombs. Even in the winter, this place was infested.

When she finished the dishes, her first move was to call Jasmine and tell her the good news.

"Hot damn, girl! What'd I tell you!"

Cece had to hold the receiver away from her ear at the volume of her friend's enthusiasm. Even so, she couldn't stop the grin that worked its way across her face.

"Yeah, ok. You told me and you were right."

"Damn straight! How're we going to celebrate? Dinner? Drinking? Dancing?"

Cece laughed. "I think I might need to build up some funds before the celebration." Jasmine's long suffering sigh from the other end of the line had her shaking her head, smile firmly in place. "Hey, at least I'm committing."

"Yeah. Guess I can't complain. Oh, girl, I'm so excited for you! Working with Cross in the big office! Which reminds me..." Her voice lowered conspiratorially as her tone turned salacious, "What did you think of him?"

For a moment, Cecilia remembered. She remembered a strong, wide chest, muscled arms she could see clearly even though his tasteful business wear and green eyes that burned into her with enough intensity to make her light-headed in want.

Jasmine hadn't been wrong. Alexander cross was by far the most delicious piece of man she'd laid eyes on in a long time.

"He's...good-looking," she finally admitted, rubbing her

thighs together in unconscious arousal, "Definitely good-looking."
 Jasmine snorted. "Honey, you have a talent for understatement."

Cristina Grenier

CHAPTER 3 - TRIAL BY FIRE

"He's a stickler for punctuality. If you're even a minute late, *thirty seconds* and he'll know. He won't be happy. This is your desk."

Cece's first day in Cross' office was a weird cross between a day-long pep talk and having to memorize an entire text book. She was, of course, led by the perpetually nervous Margaret. Cece decided the girl couldn't be a day over twenty-five and continued to examine her as she showed her to the desk in a cubicle right outside Cross' door.

"There's a new laptop. Melody took her old one with her, so this is yours." The thin girl indicated a new Macbook with slender fingers, looking over her shoulder every so often to make sure that Cross wasn't going to come barreling through the door. "You should get acquainted with Snow Leopard if you don't know it. Then, there are these."

As Cece was settling in her comfortable leather chair, Margaret knelt at her feet, revealing that every drawer in the desk was full of folders and portfolios. "Theses are all of Mr. Cross' contacts and important information on recent cases. He'll expect you to know it and be able to provide what he needs at a moment's notice." The very thought seemed to send the girl into uncontrollable shivers. "So I'd get on it. Also, here's the black book Melody left behind." She pulled out a thick, leather bound black volume in the top drawer of the desk. "All her personal contacts for getting the information Mr. Cross requires."

Though Cece was soaking up everything the girl said like a sponge, she couldn't help but be distracted by such a nervous presence. Margaret was like Xaviar when he was getting ready for an exam – twitchy, bouncy, and unbelievably paranoid.

"Margaret."

The girl jumped at shadows and, predictably, she started

when Cece interrupted her speech. Her wide blue eyes were fixed on her own, and in her gaze, Cece saw both awe and terror at the man that ran the office. "Honey, is he really that scary?"

If anything, Margaret's eyes only grew more wide. "Are you kidding me? You haven't even been here a day. You have no idea. When he barks at you...and his constant demands...I have no idea how Melody put up with it."

"Well...you seem to be holding it together...alright." Overstatement. By quite a bit. But if Cece was going to befriend the girl and have an ally in the office, the first thing she was going to have to do was calm her down.

"It hasn't even been a week. He's...he's impossible." Margaret hugged herself, shaking her head slowly back and forth like she'd been through a war zone.

"Honey, really. He's just a man. He's not God."

The God. He wasn't *the* God. *A* God was questionable. Lord knew Cross was certainly built like one.

"Cecilia, he is *here*. You'll understand soon enough."

Alright, so perhaps this would be a bit more difficult than she'd expected, but Rome wasn't conquered in a day. "Call me Cece."

Margaret only nodded stiffly before returning to her desk near the elevator bay. For the next hour or so, Cece didn't hear a peep from her, nor did Cross appear. According to Margaret, he was in his office, so Cece assumed he must not need her for anything. Perhaps that was for the best, at this juncture.

Upon looking through all the information Margaret had suggested she memorize, Cece realized she had her work cut out for her.

She was halfway through a gigantic folder containing files from a case that had gone to trial a month ago when Margaret reappeared. She was carrying a tall, slim mug of black coffee on a tray with a Danish, and she was headed straight for Cross' office. When she passed Cece's desk, the dark-skinned woman reached out and gently tapped her arm.

"Margaret."

The girl almost spilled the coffee and she stifled a groan. Standing, Cece took the tray from the poor girl before she had a conniption. "I'll take it to him."

Margaret's eyes flew wide as Cece took the tray from her. "I always take his coffee. He might be upset if I don't-"

"Margaret, honey, do me a favor, Ok?" Cece fixed the girl with her intense honey gaze. "Relax. Take a deep breath." She demonstrated by taking one of her own and, though Margaret initially gave her a funny look, the girl mirrored her next deep breath. "Good." Cece smiled warmly at her. "Now, go sit back down at your desk and take a breather. Call your boyfriend or something. I'll take the big bad Cross his breakfast in your stead."

For the first time since they'd met, a small smile appeared on the young woman's face. "Really?"

"Really really."

"Thank you...Cece." Her smile widening slightly, Margaret turned to cross back towards her desk; and as she did so, Cece noticed that the tension in her shoulders had lessened slightly. Well, that was step one.

Turning, she had to remind herself to do what she had just helped Margaret with. Doing the girl a favor was one thing, but venturing into Cross' office was quite another. Steeling herself, she maneuvered her tray so she could open the door and slip into the anteroom. From there, she quickly made her way to the man's office and knocked on the door.

"Come."

Her skin broke out in goosebumps at his low, silvery command.

When she entered, she could feel his eyes on her, measuring her mettle. Without looking at him, she crossed the room to his desk and set the tray carefully before him. The heat of him was more than enough to make her completely aware of his presence, and when she came close to him, the dark, masculine scent of him enveloped her.

"Where's Margaret?"

When she straightened, Cross's inquiry prevented her from

leaving as swiftly as she had come. Slowly, she raised her gaze to the man's face and her thighs quivered in arousal at his irate expression. He wore a gray shirt today that perfectly complimented his lake hued eyes and blonde hair. She knew the man must be in his late thirties, yet still, not a hint of gray marred his golden locks.

"I came for Margaret today. I think she needs a little breather."

A single dark brow shot up. "You think?"

Cece took a deep breath. Now, it was time to do what she did best – walk the line between diplomacy and honesty. "She's scared stiff. I think she literally believes you could strike her with lightning if the thought catches your fancy."

Cross snorted. "She needs to develop a tough skin if she wants to be an attorney. I'm hard on her because everyone else will be harder."

"That, I understand." Cece took a breath, the tips of her breasts throbbing at Cross' nearness as she continued to stand by his desk. "But consider this: She sees you as a mentor. She knows what weight your name carries and she only wants to impress you. It would mean the world to her."

The corner of his mouth kicked up in an amused smile. "Isn't your first day a bit early to try and make my heart bleed, Cecilia?"

"It might be, Mr. Cross. But it's not too early to give a jittery girl a break until the notion crosses your mind."

For a moment, the man was silent, merely staring at her with an inscrutable expression. Resting his chin on hand, he gave her a slow once over that made her shiver in its intensity. Then, leisurely, he picked up his coffee and took a sip. Cece couldn't help but imagine what his mouth might feel like on her nipple under such ministrations. "You were early this morning."

She nodded, slightly breathless. "Ten minutes."

"Hm." He took another sip of his coffee before finally looking back down to the files on his desk. "Have you been looking over the files Margaret showed you?"

Cece breathed a low sigh of relief. "Yes, sir."

"Bring me the Mason portfolio, the Trace file and any information Melody gathered in Johnathan Hughs. Then I want you to call Julia Mathers and schedule an appointment for three o'clock tomorrow. Use your discretion to book the restaurant. Then, find Ruddy Wilson and inform him that his sentence is pending. Do you have all that?"

The names meant nothing to Cece – at least not yet – but she had always had a good memory. "Mason portfolio, Trace file and Johnathan Hughs' information. Call Julia Mathers and schedule for three tomorrow. Find Ruddy Wilson and tell him about his pending sentence."

Cross nodded curtly and Cece turned to leave, only to be stopped by a firm, yet gentle grip around her upper arm. Where he touched her, intense heat arose, even through the sleeve of her suit jacket. When she looked back, she caught the full brunt of Cross' gaze and suppressed a shiver. "And tomorrow, Cecilia, you're to bring me my coffee again. At exactly eight thirty. Don't be late."

She resisted the urge to grin, instead merely nodding at her small victory. Slowly, Cross' fingers slipped from her arm and she hurried through his anteroom and back into the main office. She couldn't catch her breath until she sat down at her chair once more, and once she did, she had to force herself to calm.

The man unnerved her.

She hated to admit it, but he both unnerved and intimidated her. It was her job to never, *ever* let him know it. It was enough that she grew soft and wet between the legs at his mere touch on her arm. To let him know that he effected her emotions so vividly would be suicide.

For both her *and* Margaret.

True to the young woman's word, Cross worked her intensely for her first two weeks. Though Cece had thought Margaret might be exaggerating the extent to which Cross depended on his P.A, she soon found out the truth.

Everyday was a long day.

The tasks the man had set out for her the first day took her four hours. She was unfamiliar with the paperwork, with her new laptop and with all that was expected of her. While this made Margaret nervous, Cece only worked to make sure it would never happen again.

She took case files home with her. Though she was loathe to allow it, her new job required that she stay late at the office and so, Xaviar had to take the bus home. So far, he hadn't regaled her with any further violent stories, and so she could rest easy at night, knowing that he didn't seem to be in any imminent danger.

What did upset her was how little time she now got to spend with him. Though he assured her that he understood that she was working for his benefit, the fact that she only saw him for dinner and perhaps an hour before bed was hard to get used to. She tried not to focus on her guilt and instead tried to pack as much information as humanly possible into her head.

And there was a veritable ton.

Cross had told her what he expected before he'd hired her. It was her fault that she hadn't comprehended how difficult the adjustment from unemployed to jack-of-all-trades would be. Atop that, she got a strange sense that Cross was watching her; and not in the normal sense of an employee studying his employee.

More like a predator waiting to pounce.

Being around the man was a strain on both her nerves and her libido. If she'd thought it a trial to withstand his gaze the first morning she bought his coffee, harder still was enduring it every day after. They developed a little ritual: she brought his coffee and Danish into his office and he would sip, slowly, as he stared at her.

She, of course, was waiting for him to request what he needed of her that day. Though Margaret had told her that, before she had volunteered to take the coffee, this had usually been done by intercom, Cross took advantage of her presence to tell her directly. But, he took his time with it. He drank his coffee and stared, licked full lips as he signed off on documents and savored his danish the way she wished he would savor her body.

This would go on for about five minutes until he finally spoke with her, his tone low and authoritative. He would give her a seemingly impossible list of commands, and she would immediately start wondering how to accomplish them in a day. As she did so, she would drive from her mind all thoughts of leaping into the man's lap and offering herself up to his lusts.

She could only imagine a man like him had a big appetite.

What she could not imagine, however, was any genuine interest he might have in her. She was learning, and right now, he was testing her, bending her to see how far she could go until she snapped. Cece was taking everything he had and, in her opinion, delivering pretty admirably for someone who had never worked with him before. If he chastised her on finding a document too late, or making the wrong appointment, she corrected it immediately. The next appointment was made faster, the next document found within an hour of his requesting it.

It was a dangerous dance.

If she wanted to stay employed, she would have to impress the man – while simultaneously hiding the inexplicable, raw lust that coursed through her system whenever he was around.

It was most poignant when she questioned him. The mere notion of challenging something he asked her to do made her warm between the legs. The look he would give her – as if no one had ever second guessed him before and that to do so was a serious breach of conduct – was somehow arousing. Now, if he had ever actually admitted that she was overstepping her boundaries, she might have given up these little luxuries

But he *didn't*.

In fact, despite the way he looked at her, he seemed almost intrigued by her suggestions. Though it had taken two weeks, he did, indeed, seem to take more care in startling Margaret. When he barked, it was at her rather than at the younger woman, and Cece had been barked at before.

That wasn't what she was afraid of.

What scared her most was the idea of failing – of having to go home to Xaviar with nothing because she hadn't tried hard enough. Hell would freeze over before that happened.

And so, she worked with Cross everyday, and everyday she became more and more proficient at the job. By the end of the second week, she'd committed almost sixty perfect of his files to memory and knew her way around her Mac better than she had ever known a PC. She almost relished Cross's requests, as they were a chance to prove her prowess; and even though the man's gaze still threatened to melt her into an amorphous pool of liquid heat on the floor, she was beginning to understand him.

And that was crucial.

**

She was good.

As much as Alexander hated to admit it, Cecilia was extremely good. She'd come in with absolutely no experience, he'd put her through her paces and, incredibly, she was shining.

Her efficiency was worrisome.

Not because it jeopardized his work but because it forced him to realize that she was more than just a gorgeous face. Every day since he employed her, she marched into his office with his coffee, her head held high, eyes defiant.

She was the exact opposite of Margaret, and a completely different animal than Melody.

And she didn't seem to have any notion of how much she *tortured* him.

The swell of her breasts as she leaned over to place his morning tray, the smell of her- sweet and feminine, those honey eyes daring him to challenge her. And challenge her he had. In fact, the first time she'd brought him his drink, he'd been so wary of jumping her on the spot that the mountain of work he'd given her would have cowed even Melody.

It had been her first day, and he'd ached for her so badly that he'd sent her away with a series of not only one, but five impossible tasks. The files he'd asked her to retrieve were years old and had to be collected from archives uptown. Johnathan Hughs was a client whose case had already been won – six months ago. She would have had to dig through a mountain of client info in her database to find that particular tidbit. Julia Mathers was an old friend whom he'd ceased contact with after a drunken tumble and Ruddy? Ruddy was bound for prison after he'd broken Alexander's trust and turned curr on the police force.

She'd done it all. He'd intended to send her away for days – to give him peace of mind and time to calm the lust she inspired in the very core of him – but she'd returned in a mere four hours with all the tasks he'd requested completed.

She was both infuriating and awe-inspiring.

And she only got better as time went on.

He found himself watching her, fascinated by the speed with which she absorbed information. She worked through the entire day, barely taking a lunch break, to meet his needs. One thing she almost never did, however, was stay late in the office. At five o'clock, latest, every day, she raced off to whatever waited for her at home.

Home.

The prospect of Cecilia's home life inexplicably held great interest for Alexander. He'd never particularly wondered about how women behaved in their own homes, but watching the demon fervor with which Cecilia performed in the office, he had to wonder what she went home to.

Often, when he lay awake at night, he remembered the look she'd given him when he'd hired her – like he'd saved her from something worse than death. What could have possibly brought that out in her, if only for the barest of moments?

His father called, about a week after she'd started. Of course, the first thing the old man wanted to know was whether or not his temper had gotten the best of him and he'd beat the shit out of any criminals. For Alexander, it was enough to try and sweat his baser emotions out in the gym; baser motions that were gradually moving away from frustration and anger, and towards something else entirely.

Arousal. Intrigue. Obsession.

Of course, he wasn't going to reveal any of this to his father.

"How's that new PA working out for you?"

Alexander was watching Cece from the one way glass windows in his anteroom; they were his secret window into the goings-on of his office around him. She was bent over a thick file, chewing her lip as her eyes scanned lines of text. Slender fingers darted across the page as her heel slid in and out of her pump unconsciously. She had exposed the nape of her neck, and he itched to nip there – to bite and kiss until she melted against him.

"Alright." The words were emitted in a neutral tone, even as his erection strained at the front of his slacks. "She's no Melody, but she'll do."

Indeed, things had been a lot simpler with Melody. The woman had been straight-forward and concise. She did what he asked and her methods were sound.

It seemed as if nothing was ever straight forward with Cecilia. She did what he asked, yes, but every so often she would sneak in an inquiry, a correction that would catch him off guard. Alex was used to being king in his office. Though it hadn't always been that way, he had scrabbled and clawed his way upward to get where he was and, having won his position, he considered it sound that few people who worked for him questioned him.

Cecilia not only questioned him, she did it in a way that genuinely made him question *himself*. Before she had come into the office, Alexander had never actually considered that his behavior alone might be the reason why Margaret was such a nervous wreck. The other attorneys in the office seemed to bear it with indifference, but the truth of the matter was that he rarely spoke to them as he did to her. The girl was young and fragile, and he considered it his task to toughen her up a bit.

But, upon reflecting on Cecilia's words a few times, be began to consider going about it in a less potent manner. It made sense that perhaps the girl couldn't perform efficiently because she feared his wrath. He pulled back on his hovering over her and found that in a small two week period, she became less fearful when he approached her.

She was also as thick as thieves with his new PA. He had no idea how Cecilia had done it, but she'd somehow broken through the jittery girl's shell to reveal the efficient paralegal that lie underneath. Margaret got a lot more work done under her watchful eye and, in return, the girl helped Cecilia get through the mountain of information she had to memorize for him.

It was a shrewd move, he realized, for Cecilia to have accomplished this in a mere fourteen days of work. She had pinpointed the problem with Margaret and sought to correct it; and if her prodding corrections of him were any indication, she didn't intend to stop there.

He should be annoyed.

Alexander had been running his office in precisely his own way for almost six years and he had never had any trouble. Now, one little woman was beginning to alter the way he operated; and not just that, the way he thought in and of itself. Just two short weeks ago he had been utterly and completely dedicated to his cases. His work came home with him at night and was the first thing he thought of in the morning.

One more criminal behind bars.

One more victory to assuage a shattering past defeat.

But, gradually, *she* began to creep in. She would be there as he signed his daily paperwork, or as he took his lunch break. He would pass her in the hallway, or share an elevator with her, and he would find himself utterly enthralled by her. She hosted none of the pretension of high society Manhattan socialites and seemed to care nothing of ingratiating herself with him.

She did her job, and she did it well.

All while looking like a proverbial chocolate goddess flitting around the thirtieth floor and tempting him with cherry lips when she brought him his morning coffee.

At the beginning of week three, he woke for the first time with her name on his lips. When he came fully awake, he cursed at the throbbing erection he hosted and at his own weakness. The woman was working her way into his mind, moment by moment, until it was impossible to think straight.

Alexander took a slow, cold shower as he contemplated what to do about the problem. Of course, firing her would be the easiest and quickest solution. She'd be gone within the day and, of course, his mind would be free to return to the work that had so occupied it in the years before.

Somehow, however, he could not bring himself to be so callous.

The woman was obviously working her quite luscious behind off for a reason – one she never discussed at work, not even with Margaret.

And then, he had to consider what other connotations her leaving would produce. For one, he'd have let the most radiant creature he'd ever seen walk away without sampling her. For another, he'd have let insecurities created by lust win out over his more rational nature.

The second, in particular, he found he couldn't digest. Alexander had always been a rational creature, and he would continue to be. So far, his desire for Cecilia hadn't quite driven him mad; and upon further reflexion, he came across a solution that would prevent it from ever reaching such fervor.

He would have her.

Just once, mind you. Even the lusts Cecilia had inspired in him up until this point weren't enough to make him lose his mind completely. He knew that any repeat instance of romance between them would be toxic to both the atmosphere in the office and his own mind. But once...once was negotiable. They were both mature adults. Surely he hadn't been the only one to sense the electric attraction between them.

If he could feel the soft slide of her dark, soft form against him – taste those full lips and feel her writhe in ecstasy beneath him just once, then she'd stop haunting him. Though he'd never encountered a hunger so insistent before, he'd met women who tempted them with their bodies. After said bodies had been sampled, it was almost if they didn't exist. He was far too busy to follow up with the courtesy of flowers and phone calls.

For him it was, and always would be, just sex.

In the middle of the third week of her employment, Alexander found himself watching her again. Though he loathed to admit it, he passed a valuable hour of work every day straying out to the anteroom of his office to stare at her. Today she was wearing a modestly cut navy dress that easily reached her knees. All Alexander could concentrate on, however, was what the dress covered. While it was clear that Cecilia made a concerted effort to dress modestly for work every day, his mind had no problem undressing her – imagining the full breasts and dusky nipples she hid behind high cut collars; or the lush thighs well wrapped in calf length skirts.

Growling lowly in his throat, he narrowed his eyes in frustration.

But, he could blame no one but himself. He had hired her knowing exactly what effect she had on him – and it had only gotten worse. Smoothing his hair back from his brow, the district attorney turned from the enticing vision before him, stalking back into his office.

For about an hour or so, he managed to bury himself in a particularly nasty case involving the murder of eight year old twin girls. The defending attorney was a slick, dastardly piece of work and Alexander didn't want there to be any chance of the criminal getting off with anything less than a double life sentence.

Just a month ago, such a case would have consumed his every waking moment. Now, he could only concentrate for short stints of time before his mind drifted back to his alluring PA.

At that moment, his intercom buzzed, drawing his glare.

Slowly, he reached out to depress the receive button. "Yes, Cecilia." The name rolled off his tongue, leaving a rich taste in his mouth.

"Mr. Cross, there's a Madeline Everett here to see you."

He made sure to let go of the receive button before cursing lowly. Somehow, he, the master of all scheduling, had forgotten about his appointment with Mrs. Everett. She planned to make him the guest of honor at her upcoming charity event and, had he been in a better frame of mind, he would have been busy trying to find ways to thwart her.

As it was, he had nothing.

"Send her in."

He would have to be cordial – but then again, half of his career was based on cordial interactions when he'd much rather barricade himself in his office until the apocalypse drove him out. Alexander had no choice but to steel himself for the arrival of Mrs. Everett.

As always, she was charming; it was a charm that came from having money and spending it endlessly. Usually, he wouldn't tolerate such people. While he'd never been poor growing up, people who flaunted their money disgusted him. How could they be so ignorant as to parade around in their diamonds and furs when fourteen percent of the city's population was unemployed? However, Madeline was different.

Yes, she was rolling in dough and yes, she could ooze saccharine sweetness intense enough to make his stomach turn, but every year, she donated over five million dollars to one of the biggest charities in New York. For the past few years, he'd managed to duck out of attending. He hadn't had to make very many excuses – anyone who knew him knew his schedule and his vendetta.

This year, however, the woman would not be swayed. She wheedled, complimented and begged until Alexander's head was throbbing, and when he finally got rid of her, she was fully expecting to see him at her charity ball in a week with a plus one.

The thought made him cringe.

Issue atop issue. He was behind in his work, horny out of his mind, and now he was being forced to attend a social function. He would have to add it to the few on his list that he had to be part of every year to ensure that his network remained strong.

He resisted the urge to pour himself a stiff drink.

Plus one? Where the hell was he going to get a plus one?

"Mr. Cross?" His head jerked upward and he whirled to

see Cecilia silhouetted in his doorway. The sight of her creamy caramel skin and heart shaped mouth was almost more than he could take at the moment. A slender hand held out a file for his perusal. "For the Miller case." With the twin girls. He didn't remember telling her to help him source any additional information yet.

"The Miller case?" He arched a brow, reaching out slowly to take the folder from her. "What have you found?"

"A couple of prior offenses he got off for that weren't in his record. 'Erased', if you will, by a higher up. I had to do some digging, but here they are. Fuel for your fire."

Christ, he wanted nothing more than to have her here and now.

"Have dinner with me." The words escaped him before he could meter them and the moment they reached his ears, Alexander cursed himself inwardly. He sounded like some kind of desperate fool. Luckily for him, Cecilia didn't seem to have heard him correctly.

"Excuse me?" Her honey eyes were narrowed in confusion.

Clearing his throat, Alexander made another go of it – far cleaner this time. "To commemorate your being here three weeks. I thought we might have dinner. There's an impeccable French restaurant only a few blocks away."

For a moment, the young woman's eyes studied him thoroughly. So far, in the time they'd worked together, Alexander had contained himself. He hadn't let the slightest hint of his attraction to her slip. Who knew? Perhaps he'd come to his senses in the next several hours and the dinner would actually *be* a business outing.

"I...I need to get home." Her answer was evident, and for the first time since he'd hired her, Alexander found that she would not meet his gaze. "Right after work."

He should have let it go.

The *smart* thing to do would have been to let it go; however, if he'd done that, he didn't know if he would have the wherewithal to keep from doing something idiotic in the office. If he was going to lose himself, he'd rather it be outside the vicinity, on his terms.

Always on his terms.

"Perhaps we can leave a bit early then. Around four? We'll arrive just before the rush and can enjoy our food before you return home."

Now, Cecilia's eyes were wide. "Leave work early? You?"

His eyes narrowed at her attempt at humor. "Need I remind you that I'm your boss?"

Her lips quirked slightly and he was very aware that she knew of the idleness of his threat. There were very few he'd be able to find that could do work with her efficiency – another thing he found hard to admit.

"No, you don't need to remind me. Are you *ordering* me to dinner then?" The imperious cock of her hips made his fingers itch to curl into them.

"I'm requesting."

She looked up at him for a long beat and Alexander was almost certain she'd refuse him. Then, all at once, she sighed, shaking her head. "I suppose it would be nice...I haven't been out to eat in ages..." As the statement slipped from her lips, she covered her mouth, her expression alarmed. Before he could inquire what bothered her, she simply turned from him to flee his office. "I'll see you at four then."

Alexander stared after her, stepped in a mixture of confusion and arousal. What had that been? If she preferred to have dinner at home, why should that be any of his business? He sincerely hoped she didn't assume that he was some monied socialite who judged those of different social classes. The people that depended upon him were of all social classes, and he turned no one away for inability to pay.

Justice, as cliché as it sounded, was priceless.

He sank into the chair behind his desk, his fingers tented against one another as he contemplated. That was it then. She'd agreed to come with him for dinner. Now, he had a few hours to

Cristina Grenier

decide how much of a gentleman he was going to be.

CHAPTER 4 - CLOSE ENCOUNTERS

Slightly in awe, Cece glanced at the restaurant they'd just stepped into, trying not to gape. While she was no stranger to fine dining, this place was something out of this world. Finely crafted chandeliers hung from the ceiling of the small space, illuminating it with low, soft light. The décor was done in hues of soft peach and lavender and smelled absolutely heavenly. Elegant booths wound their way around the perimeter of the room white a few small tops draped with tablecloths filled the center of the floor.

All in all, the restaurant could probably seat only about thirty people, lending it a cozy, intimate atmosphere. When she and Alexander entered, he was greeted in French. Cece had to fight to keep her cool as her employed responded fluently in the language, his low tones caressing the foreign syllables like a lover.

Where the hell had he learned to speak French?

It was one of many questions that had risen in her head ever since she'd left his office in a hurry that morning.

He wanted to take her to dinner - to commemorate her work in the office, he'd said. Normally, Cece would see straight through such an obvious come on, but Cross had never been anything more than professional with her. Sure, sometimes he stared at her for longer than was customary, but she was pretty certain that was more to intimidate her that it spoke to any heat between them.

Of course, every time his intense green gaze fell upon her, she was scalded by it. How many hours had she spent working at her desk trying not to imagine her employer working only ten feet away?

Dinner.

Regardless of the reason, she would be alone with him – a man. Therefore, it was very hard for Cece to separate the idea from that of a date. Of course, she'd never been on a date with a man as influential or gorgeous as him but here she was, in a fancy French restaurant, letting him lead her to a quiet table in the back.

She should feel guilty.

Even if she did finish her dinner in the next hour, she'd be late getting home to Xaviar. That was less time that she'd get to spend with him, ultimately. However, when Cross had asked her, his voice low, smooth and sure, she hadn't been able to say no. At the very least, perhaps she'd be able to catch a few secret glimpses of the man that she could treasure when she was alone.

God knew she'd been doing enough treasuring to the feelings he inspired in her.

All she had to do was keep her cool throughout this dinner. It was business, as he'd said. It was not a date; rather, it was a kindness he was showing her. A kindness that, almost a month ago, she was sure Margaret wouldn't have been willing to believe he would extend.

But the man wasn't all cold, hard work ethic.

One could tell as much simply by looking over his hierarchy of cases. Cross always worked his most difficult prosecution first; like the Miller case. Cece herself could remember the chill that had come over her as she'd watched the news report. Walter Miller was a monster. He'd raped and murdered two girls before trying to dump their bodies in the Hudson and he'd been caught! She'd thought there would be no question – the man would be put to death, or life at least.

However, less harsh punishments were being discussed.

Cross was working day in and day out to make sure that justice was served and had placed the case at the top of his list. Despite the fact that he'd implied that Cece couldn't make his heart bleed, she was pretty sure it already did.

So now, she was seated in front of her wickedly attractive, deeply complicated boss, wondering how she was going to hold her own for the next hour.

"Do you have French often?" He was looking at her over the top of the menu, his deep green eyes intense on her face.

Cece flushed. To be honest, she'd never been to a French restaurant, especially not in her current financial state - but hell would freeze over before she'd admit that to him.

"Not...not very. I don't think I know what to order." She picked up her own menu to avoid the heat of his gaze and began to scan it. Nothing looked familiar to her. Half of the entrees were in a language she couldn't even begin to understand. Christ, even when she couldn't see him, she could still smell him.

Cross smelled exactly as a man should smell -sharp and male - and even catching a whiff of him in the corridor was enough to make her thighs tingle. "Perhaps we should start with a bottle of wine."

Oh, no. That wasn't a very good idea at all. She'd never been very good at holding her liquor.

"I, um...have to drive home."

"Your car is in the office parking garage, right? I'll cover your overnight ticket and call you a cab."

And just like that, the decision was made. Cece knew she should be irritated by the man's overbearing demeanor, but instead, she found that it merely fueled her arousal. As Margaret had told her, he ruled his office with an iron grip. There were, however...other things she'd prefer him to have an iron grip on...

Christ. She was out of her mind. Jasmine was very obviously rubbing off on her. As Cross gestured over a waiter to order the wine, she took a deep breath, trying to calm herself. She just needed to act natural – calm. She'd only have a glass or two of wine, and she'd make sure to eat enough to absorb the alcohol.

Cece would later admit that she hadn't stuck to her self-imposed plan very well. When the wine came, she immediately gulped down her first glass, hoping it would calm her nerves. Cross' insistent, protracted stares in the office were one thing. For him to continue watching her as she attempted to keep her cool when they were alone was another entirely.

"So, you're adjusting to the office well then?" Cross' question caught her slightly off guard as she continued to scan the menu, hoping to make sense of something. She raised her gaze, nodding with a small smile that she hoped was satisfactory.

"It's a lot of information to remember, but I think I'm getting the hang of it."

"Good." The way the man's lips moved over the edge of his wine glass was divine. "I have to say: the position's not for everyone. I'm glad you're adjusting quickly. It makes for more efficiency."

Of course. Efficiency. Cross was, after all, a man who put his work before everything else. Cece nodded at his statement, blinking as he poured her another glass of wine. She'd had no idea that she'd downed the first one so quickly.

Whatever variety he'd chosen, the taste was smooth and sweet, unlike drier red wines she's had before. "What kind of wine is this?"

His lips quirked slightly at her inquiry. "A Cabernet. Twenty year. One of my favorites." He was now pouring himself another glass with relish, and Cece realized that half the bottle had gone – just like that. "Do you like wine, Cecilia?" It was arresting, the way he said her name. Cece hadn't had anyone call her by her full name since her mother had been alive. Of course, Xaviar used it sometimes to tease her, but on the whole, it had been ages since she'd heard it used in proper context.

She decided that she liked the sound of it – at least, the way Cross presented it.

By the time she realized that she had missed the question he'd asked her, it was far too late to recover. Instead, she merely flushed slightly, hoping that she hadn't given too much away. "I'm – I'm sorry?"

"Do you like wine?" He repeated in a fluid tone, making her suppress a shudder at the silky timbre of is voice.

"It's not bad..."

"You like cocktails, I assume?": He inquired with a raised brow that made her cringe slightly. Christ, the man couldn't possibly judge her for the drinks she preferred, could he?

"Sometimes..." She managed in recovery. "Though, to tell the truth, I really don't drink much, usually."

Righting Wrongs

"Well then, I suppose we should order food. Wouldn't want you too far gone to enjoy it." The large man plucked the menu from where it lay in front of her, gesturing to the waiter once more. Cece really didn't have much choice but to let him order for her. At this point, she was desperate to get something on her stomach – anything. If she didn't...well, her mouth might get carried away with her.

She tried not to listen to him speak french when the impeccably tailored waiter returned to their table side. If she concentrated on her wine, it was almost possible.

Almost.

"Where did you learn French?" It was the only thing she could think of to ask once they were alone once more. Cross tossed back the rest of his wine before fixing her with his intense green stare.

"My mother taught me when I was younger. Her mother was French, and so she wouldn't accept her daughter being unable to speak her language. A pet peeve she passed on to me."

It must be nice, Cece mused, to have normal parents and a normal childhood. If the only thing she'd had to worry about was her father pushing her to learn a foreign language, she'd have been in hog heaven. Instead, she'd had to worry about the man trying to sell her off for drugs, or sending her down to the corner store to try and steal beers for him.

She was glad Xaviar had never had to face such things.

"Are you alright, Cecilia?" Her head jerked up at Cross' sudden inquiry and she realized her bitterness must have shown on her face. The man was gazing at her almost as if he were worried about her, and his expression gave her pause.

She was the man's PA. Without her, undoubtedly, he'd have a difficult time getting through his casework. That would be the only reason he might care if she was out of sorts.

"I'm OK. Just...just hungry is all."

"Are you certain it's just hunger?" The way his tongue moved over the word, molding and shaping it like it were a piece of darkly sweet chocolate, made her want to swoon.

She had to get out of here. She was losing her head.

"I – excuse me, for a moment." She rose for the table abruptly, hurrying towards the ladies room.

Once inside, she splashed water on her heated face, berating herself.

Grow up Cece.

She stared at her image in the mirror. She was tall, she was capable, and she was strong. All the wine was rushing to her head and that was what was stealing all her sanity away. She *just* needed to get through thirty minutes more with the man. Then, she could take a cab home and indulge in whatever blissful fantasies she'd cooked up.

"Keep it together." She whispered lowly to herself as she washed her hands. "Just a bit more. Keep it *together* girl."

Steeling herself, she straightened her spine and lifted her head into the air to stalk back out of the bathroom.

"Are you *certain* you're alright?" She had hardly taken two steps from the safety of the ladies room before she jumped, whirling to see Cross waiting for her just beyond the partition. Before she could answer, the man advanced on her, taking her arm in a firm but gentle grip that sent shivers down her spine. "You're acting strange, Cecilia. Are you sick?"

He raised his opposite hand to rest his palm on her forehead as if she was a child, checking for her temperature. Immediately wary of so intimate a gesture, she jerked back, a bit breathless. In her nervousness, the word she spoke came out harsher than she'd intended.

"*Don't.*"

For a moment, the man just towered over her, staring down at her with an unreadable expression. He was tall – impossibly tall – breathtakingly gorgeous, and he practically oozed the confidence of a man used to getting his way.

It was like her hormones were crying out for him to take her. "'Don't' what?"

"Touch me." The words escaped her before she could prevent them. And once she started, to her embarrassment, Cece found that she couldn't stop. "Don't touch me again. I can't take it."

Thank God there were the only ones in the restaurant. Even with her low tone of voice, she would have been making a scene otherwise. Cross, however, only stared down at her, his expression slightly bemused. "My apologies, Miss Thompson. I had no idea you found me so revolting."

A short bark of laughter escaped her. Revolting? *Revolting?*

"Cross, you'll have to pardon my bluntness, but you're an *idiot* if you don't know what effect you have on women. I'm your PA, alright? I'm trying to do the best I can with the cards I've been dealt and you...you're just...messing me up!"

"Messing you up?" Now, the man's brow was cocked in what could only be amusement.

"Yes!" Alcohol fueled her words as she continued. "Every day that I come in, you're there in your perfectly tailored suits with that huge body and that ridiculously swarthy visage. I'm trying to do my job and you're just... *distracting!*"

"Distracting?"

"Yes!"

"*I'm* distracting?"

"Hell yes!"

God, she was so fired. All it had taken was two glasses of wine and she'd *way* overstepped her boundaries. Jasmine was going to kill her. Her friend had gone out of her way to secure this position for her and she had squandered it with her own carelessness. And what was she going to tell Xaviar? She'd promised him he could go to a better school in a year.

"Cecilia Thompson." At Cross' low, husky tone, her eyes widened. She took a step back as he took one forward, repeating the motion until her back was flush against the wall separating the bathroom from the dining room. Cross couldn't be more than scant inches from her. "You have no *idea* what distracting is."

Then, suddenly and *completely* without warning, the man's mouth was on hers.

Cece's sharp gasp of surprise was swallowed as he kissed her – and *what* a kiss.

His lips were full and firm as they moved over hers, sending sparks shooting down her spine. When his tongue slid against the seam of her mouth in a entreaty for her lips to part, she hardly hesitated. The dexterous muscle surged into her mouth, moving brusquely against hers so a low, shuddering moan escaped her. He tasted like wine, coffee and sheer masculinity – spicy and so intoxicating that she was lightheaded with it.

Her hands automatically liften to his shoulders as she rose onto her toes, meeting every thrust of his tongue with one of her own until a low, throbbing ache settled between her legs. The man's arms encircled her waist, bolstering her with their strength as the kiss went on and on... Cece wasn't entirely certain she minded if she ever breathed again. She was hyper-aware of the hardness of his body against her own soft curves and wanted, more than anything, to feel the slide of his bare body over her skin.

When the kiss finally ended, Cross drawing back and she struggling to catch her breath, Cece's entire body was aflame.

When her eyes met Cross' the intensity of the lust she found there made her tremble slightly, her lips parted in shock.

All this time...*all* this time, he'd wanted her as much as she'd wanted him?

"You look so surprised." His voice was low and sinuous, sending liquid lust rushing through her veins. "Do you really think I have you bring my coffee every morning just to give Margaret a reprieve?"

This was wrong. This man was her boss and she was committing the most egregious faux paus in the book by letting him touch her this way; but *damn* if it didn't feel good. "You want me." Her voice was surprisingly steady, considering how unsteady she was on her feet.

"I aim to have you." He replied, his eyes burning into hers. "Unless you tell me no."

Christ.

She'd barely worked in his office for three weeks and now she was going to sleep with the man. Every rational part of her brain, even dulled by alcohol as they were, protested against such action. She would be putting her position in jeopardy – she could lose the income that promised to extract her and Xaviar from the brink of poverty. "Promise me one thing..." She managed to breathe, her nipples tingling against the steel-like pane of his chest.

"Name it." His low growl worked hard to make her forget her demand, but Cece wasn't going to let all her hard work go to waste.

"Just once." Her honey colored eyes searched his desperately. He was Manhattan's avenging angel of the law; he had to know how devastating this could be for their working relationship – for his position - if it got out of hand; never mind how devastating the loss of this job would be to her. "And no one ever knows."

"Once." He affirmed with a curt nod of his head. " Our secret."

Slowly, she nodded. This time, he didn't catch her so off guard when he kissed her; but that didn't mean the hunger of his mouth against hers didn't send her reeling. The man drank from her mouth as if she was water in a desert, as if she tasted finer, even, than the expensive bottle of wine he'd ordered. Cece was still dazed when he drew back, releasing his hold on her waist only to encircle her hand in his larger one and draw her towards the door of the restaurant.

He called something in French to the waiter, who only nodded politely in deference, before they were outside, the chill winter air whipping through her hair. To her surprise, Cross pulled her behind his huge body, shielding her from the chill as they walked back towards the office building.

His car was parked on the fourth level of the parking deck – a brilliant black Mercedes that took her breath away. Despite the hot lust driving her forward, she paused for a moment to look over it in awe. "Your car is *gorgeous*."

She inhaled sharply as the man's breath came hotly against her ear, a very prominent bulge pressing against the small of her back. "There's hardly room to do what I plan in the car, Cecilia." His hand swatted against her behind firmly, making her jump at the slight sting. "It's a means to an end."

Her face flushing, the woman hurried forward to slide into the passenger seat the moment he unlocked the vehicle. Classical music burst to life from the speakers as he skillfully maneuvered out of his parking space and into the busy streets.

As he drove, Cece tried to come to terms with what was about to happen. She was going home with her boss. She had agreed on a one time encounter – just to clear both of their minds from the rampant lust that seemed to be guiding them. She was still reeling from the fact that the man had admitted he'd wanted her from day one. She'd thought such a thing impossible. She wasn't his type – how could she compete with perfect, skinny, blonde, monied socialites?

She glanced over at his profile, from strong chin and biceps stretching his suit jacket to perfectly slicked back blonde locks and full mouth; Christ, women must be crawling all over themselves to get to him.

But he was hers. Even if just for one evening, she had him all to herself.

They didn't speak as he drove; instead, the tension crackled thickly through the car and Cece found herself licking her lips in anticipation.

His apartment was on the upper east side; a posh looking building with a well dressed doorman who greeted him by name as they entered. They took the elevator to the thirtieth floor, and when she chanced a look over in the man's direction, she found him staring at her with such hot intensity that she blushed.

His apartment made her drafty, decrepit place in Brooklyn look like a roach motel. High ceilings, a state of the art kitchen, a huge living room with full entertainment center and a hallway leading off to God knew how many more rooms. The moment she was inside, Cece felt a bit intimidated. Though she'd once had money, she'd never been anywhere near this well off; and the splendor of the flat was making her a bit nervous.

She stood by the door, fingering the strap of her purse idly as Cross dropped his keys in a small bowl on a table by the door and then shucked his suit jacket before tossing it over the back of the couch. When he turned back to see her standing just beyond the doorway, he arched a brow. "Changed your mind?"

For a moment, Cece stared at him.

He intimidated her, yes; him and his money and his power. But she hadn't let him cow her in the office. Why should she let him do it now? Without a word, she dropped her purse on the table as well and slid her own threadbare coat from her shoulders. It joined Cross' on the couch before she strode over to him. As he watched her advance, the man's lips curved into a wicked smile that made her knees weak.

When she reached him, he took her wrist in a firm grip, turning her form to back her against the nearest wall. When she couldn't take another step, his arms enveloped her and his mouth fused against hers once more. Cece rose onto her toes to more firmly slant her mouth against his and he groaned, low in his throat, as she nipped at his lips teasingly.

She gasped as he bent to slide his hands under her thighs, lifting her into the air effortlessly to settle himself between her legs, deepening the kiss. Though he was still entirely clothed, Cece could feel the hard length of his arousal jutting against her core; and the heat of it made her breathless. The man ground himself against her, pressing her into the wall so she gasped at the bolt of pure sensation that streaked through her. She arched against, him, tearing her mouth from his, only to have him turn his attentions to the line of her neck and throat.

When his lips found the sensitive skin there, she shuddered. The man nipped and licked down the length of the long column until he found the hollow at its base. When his tongue slid into the niche there, she shuddered, her fingers rising to tangle in his silky blonde locks. Then, he was kissing her again, hungry demand in every thrust of his tongue against hers. She hardly noticed him carrying her deftly down the long hall until he was edging the door at the end open, revealing a massive bedroom.

He crossed the length of it to lower her onto the bed before kicking off his shoes and beginning to loosen the tie at his throat. When Cece moved to help him, he stopped her with a single command.

"No." He slipped his tie over his head, tossing it onto the floor as he began on the buttons of his shirt. His eyes, however, never left hers – the raw lust there making her faint with its intensity. "You stay right where you are."

As if she could move.

Cece's legs were jelly from his kisses and caresses; and in this particular moment, she couldn't tear her eyes away from the god-like man undressing before her. He shucked his shirt as quickly as he had his tie, and beneath it, the network of muscle and sinew that Cece had only dreamed about was revealed. The man's arms were hard and sculpted, his chest massive in width. Though she knew that it was a common belief that most lawyers were pencil-necked nerds, Cross was obviously living proof that such assumptions were false. She stared at him unabashedly, his strong abdomen stretching the thin material of the t-shirt he wore.

She had to touch him.

Cece reached for him, only to have the man take both her wrists in a firm grip. One of his knees dipped onto the bed as he leaned over her, pinning her arms on either side of her head in a smooth motion. "Just as headstrong here as in the office, I see." He smirked down at her, making her insides clench in anticipation. "I'll make you obey me, Cecilia; one way or the other."

Any way. *All* ways. She was willing to endure anything at this point, as long as it culminated in him inside of her. "Now...don't move." He released her wrists to draw large hands slowly over the length of her body. Even though Cece was completely clothed, his touch scalded her through the fabric – skating over her breasts, molding her hips and roving the curves of her thighs. Without warning, the man quickly rolled her over so she was lying on her stomach. Slowly, she felt the zipper of her dress being drawn down along the length of her spine – tooth by tooth. She'd chosen this dress, as well as the rest of her office attire, because it was modest. High neckline, knee length skirt – she'd never been the type to distract with her body on the job.

Apparently, her efforts hadn't worked on Cross.

No sooner had he unzipped her dress than Cece felt the heat of his mouth at the small of her back, making her gasp. He blazed a trail of kisses up the length of her spine that had her shuddering before nipping and sucking at the back of her neck. "I've watched you bent over that desk..."He murmured huskily against her skin, "And I'll I wanted to do was ravage you...here." he bit down at the juncture of her neck and shoulder and Cece moaned.

"*Cross...*"

All at once, the careful bun she'd concocted from her rampant curls that morning was taken in a firm grip. She gasped as her head was drawn back - not enough to hurt, but enough to remind her exactly who she was dealing with.

"Call me by my name."His opposite hand lifting her chin to look up at him, Alexander Cross met her gaze. "What's my name, Cecilia?" His hips pressed forward, bringing the ridge of his erection flush against her clothed womanhood and Cece trembled, biting back a whimper at the size and heat of him.

"A-Alexander."

"Good girl." He reached beneath her, shoving the sleeves of the dress from her arms so she was forced to abandon the top half of her dress. Beneath it, she wore a simple black cotton bra, her breasts nearly spilling from the restraining garment. Alexander then released his hold on her, turning her over onto her back once more to face him.

The man above her was majestic, muscles flexing, expression burning with barely repressed lust as he looked down upon her scantily clad chest. Cece could feel her arousal beginning to soak though her panties as the man lowered his hands to cup her full breasts almost reverently. Cece knew this was only supposed to be a one time thing, but she never would have imaged Alexander Cross would be a man to take his time. She'd thought he'd strip her, fuck her, and then be done with it.

Instead, he appeared to be...savoring her.

He massaged the full globe of a breast in each hand before reaching for her bra straps. Within moments, they were down around her waist, the rest of her bra following suit so her chest was bared to his gaze. Though she was no untried virgin, Cece found herself blushing now at the intensity of his gaze. She'd always known that she was well endowed – in middle and high school, she'd been teased for her curves.

Cross seemed to have an entirely different opinion.

Without a word, he lowered his head to her breasts to take the taut peak of a nipple into his mouth. As hot, drugging suction enveloped the peak of her breast, Cece cried out, her fingers immediately tangling in his hair in an attempt to draw him closer. His free hand worked at her opposite breast, plumping and tweaking at its aureole as he suckled at her, making the dark-skinned woman squirm.

Cross groaned against her hot flesh, increasing his administrations until the bead of flesh between his teeth was so hard it hurt. Then, he moved onto its twin, giving it the same treatment. Cece bit her lip, her back arching into the divine sensation his mouth provided. Christ, it had been far too long since she'd felt anything like this.

Since she'd *allowed* herself to let go like this.

"Sweet." Her lover's voice was a low, sinuous murmur as he finally released her nipple with a faint *pop*. "You're so goddamn sweet, Cecilia..." His mouth continued to forge a path downwards, over her stomach and inexorably towards the crux of her thighs. As he trekked southward, cross yanked the bottom half of her dress over her hips and off, tossing it carelessly to the floor.

Now, she was left clad only in her dark cotton panties, the fabric gleaming with excited moisture.

He teased her. Just before his mouth reached her pelvic

bone, Alexander diverted. He laved each of her hipbones with his tongue, making her shiver, before trailing paths of small, stinging bites down both of her inner thighs, alternating between left and right as he went. When his breath finally fell on the core of her, Cece thought she would go insane. She arched her hips in a wordless plea, only to gasp when the man's hands curled brusquely into her bare behind holding her in place.

"Look at me."

The dark-haired woman flushed darkly at the prospect but did as he said. When her gaze met his, her heart hammered in her chest at the stern look on his face. "I am taking my *time*." His tongue lingered on the word, emphasizing it. "You don't set the pace here. I do. Understand?"

Breathless, she nodded.

Were it any other man – *any* other – she hardly would have stood to be ordered around. But Cross' firm grip and his commanding tone demanded submission – and intense arousal. However, when the man yanked her hips from the edge of the bed, she couldn't help the cry of surprise that escaped her. Strong arms held her pelvis aloft as he knelt on the carpet, his mouth ghosting over the edges of her panties. Cece had never been one for skimpy underwear, but this once, she wished she had worn her tiniest thong. Cross' heated breath so close to where she needed it most was driving her out of her mind.

Her toes curled as his tongue traveled over the moist length of her slit, tasting her through her drenched cotton panties. He shifted her hips in his grip enough to take hold of her underwear, peeling them down her legs to cast aside. Then, she was completely naked. Cece had only the barest fraction of a moment to be self-conscious - to dwell on her laundry list of imperfections – before his mouth closed over her clitoris.

Her back arched, her fists clenching in the bedclothes as she bit her lip against a cry of pleasure. Despite the way her hips twisted, Alexander's hold remained firm. He sucked on her powerfully before his tongue circled the bud of a pleasure, drawing a shuddering moan from her. Then, the dexterous, slick muscle slid over the length of her opening before sliding within her.

The cry she'd been withholding suddenly burst from her as Cece's entire body trembled. Christ, the man's mouth was as thorough as it was devastating, stimulating her until she was faint with the pleasure of it. The motions of his tongue were slow and deliberate, making her shudder as he stimulated her leisurely. She grasped at the sheets, the bedpost, anything to keep her grounded as he ate at her, relishing her as if she were some sort of rich dessert.

Finally, she couldn't take it anymore. "*Alexander!*" Her inner muscled clenched spasmodically as pleasure threatened to overtake her. "Jesus, Alexander, *please!*"

In response, he merely increased his efforts and a loud cry escaped her as she came suddenly, almost violently, her entire body taut as a bowstring. She was still shaking when Cross eased her up onto the bed, crawling onto it to lean over her. His sinful tongue swiped over his full mouth, cleaning his lips of her juices.

"I'm not *pleasing* you, Cecilia?" His mouth pressed against her jaw, her ear and then her neck as she caught her breath. "Are my methods not satisfactory?" His fingers found the wet slickness between her legs, manipulating her swollen folds expertly. Cece gasped, sensation streaking up her spine at his ministrations.

"*Alexander...*" Her voice came out a breathless moan as she caught his face in her hands, drawing it down to mold her lips to his. She tasted herself on his lips and found the flavor intoxicating, her tongue sliding against his. Cross allowed her a moment of indulgence before lifting his mouth from hers and firmly pulling her higher up on the bed.

He stripped his t-shirt over his head and for a moment, and Cece marveled at the intricate musculature of his chest; and then he was working at his slacks, sliding them down well formed legs. When he returned to her, he was completely naked, and Cece's mouth was dry with wanting him. The hot, hard length of his erection skimmed over her stomach, making the muscles there contract in anticipation.

Reaching up, he pulled at the band that held her hair in place, spilling her dark curls over the pillow. "Like this..." He murmured huskily, drawing his hand almost reverently over her cheek before his fingers caressed her lips. "It was just like this."

"Like what?" She inquired softly, unable to look away from his concentrated green gaze. Cece inhaled sharply as he took a handful of her curls, drawing them taut as he lifted one of her long legs over his shoulder, parting her for him.

"Like this." His growl was almost primal as he thrust home into her wet sheath, making her gasp at the size of him. He filled her deliciously and intimately, stretching her inner passage to its limits as she clutched at the pillows for purchase. His gaze still firm on her hair, Alexander set a slow, mind-numbing rhythm, each stroke making her gasp with the power behind it. With one hand on her thigh and the other tangled in her mussed curls, he held her firmly in place. She couldn't have escaped the depth of his thrusts if shed wanted to.

Cece whimpered and moaned, his languid cadence torturing her. Each movement of him within her stimulated her until she thought she would lose her mind. Alexander's low sounds of pleasure resonated through her, her toes curling as he angled upward to touch a place within her that made her see stars. She felt her body winding tighter and tighter as she was drawn towards her second peak of the evening and inhaled sharply, arching her hips in an attempt to have him even deeper. When she shifted, Alexander cursed lowly, the muscles in his shoulders tightening as his rhythm dissolved and he pressed deep inside her rapidly – hungrily.

Cece's orgasm crashed over her with enough force to leave her breathless, her head falling back as she clung to the pillows to keep herself grounded. The pleasure seemed to go on for an eternity, sizzling along her nerve endings until her body was left absolutely boneless against the coverlet. Groaning loudly, Alexander soon followed suit, his sweat slick body glistening as he flooded her inner passage with the warmth of his completion.

For a moment, neither of them moved.

As Cece came back to herself, she stared at the ceiling, her body still thrumming with her lover's presence. When Alexander moved, it was to extricate himself from her, making her gasp as he slid from her tender passage. She knew at once that she would be sore the next day. Forget whatever rumors there were about black men being well-endowed- Alexander had been blessed with more than his share and he knew how to wield it.

He slipped from the bed without a sound and strode, naked, across the room to disappear into what she presumed was a bathroom. As soon as the door had shut behind him, Cece sat up as guilt and worry started to creep in.

Christ.

Christ.

What had she done? A couple of drinks and she'd let Alexander take her to bed with hardly any hesitation at all! Granted, she'd been attracted to the man for a long while, but what had she been thinking? She was going to have to go back to work with him.

And every time she saw his face, all she would be able to remember was his expression when he'd slipped inside her...the way his mouth had wreaked havoc between her legs...

She covered her face with her hands, taking a deep breath. She just had to pull herself together. Though she'd been drunk, she had had enough presence of mind to insist that intimacy between them happen just once. They were both consenting adults, weren't they? They could get over this.

She rose from the bed, quickly finding her underwear and sliding into them. She had gotten her dress over her hips and was shrugging into the bodice when Cross reappeared, still sans a stitch of clothing. When her gaze met his, she froze, mid-action.

Only moments ago she had been all to eager for him to see her unclad; now she wanted nothing more than to get dressed as quickly as possible – to retain her dignity and her employment. It was hard, however, when the man was advancing on her, all rippling muscles and erection at half mast.

"Cross..." Before she could say anything more, she was in

Righting Wrongs

his arms. He kissed her, and all rational thought fled. As his hands shoved her dress back to the floor, she made a lame attempt at protest. "Cross, I have to go-"

"What have I told you about using my name?" His hands curled into the full globes of her behind, squeezing possessively. His erection pressed against her stomach, making her knees weak as new lust slammed into her with the force of a hurricane.

"Alexander, I have to go." Her words were weak, trembling as he hastened to free her breasts once more. Once the swollen, heavy flesh was released, he palmed her bosom eagerly, his mouth on her jaw.

"You use birth control?"

"Yes, but-" She cried out as his teeth nipped at the peak of her breast before laving it with moisture from his tongue. Then, she was spun around and marched back to the bed, where she was bent over brusquely. Her panties fell down her legs, and the next thing she knew, Alexander slid into her from behind, He thrust so deep Cece swore she could feel him up to her brain. She shrieked, clawing at the mattress.

Cross growled, grinding his hips against hers so the world went white around her. Then he settled into a demanding rhythm, not exploring, not sampling, but *fucking* her until his body and his cock were the only things she was cognizant of. She should have stopped him, should have pushed him away – should have reminded him of their deal, but instead all she could do was gasp and moan for more.

It didn't look like she was set to return home anytime soon.

Cristina Grenier

CHAPTER 5 - Secrets

She was late.

Alexander checked the clock on his desk for the umpteenth time in the last minute and frowned. It was eight minutes past eight. Not one day in her three week employment had Cecilia arrived anything less than ten minutes early.

He'd told Margaret to buzz him the instant she arrived and his intercom remained silent.

He'd been an ass.

Alexander had known the moment he laid hands on Cecilia that he wouldn't be able to keep his promise. Her skin was warm and pliant beneath his fingers, her lips soft and lush – and the sounds she made when he touched her? The man emitted a pained groan at the mere memory.

He'd been with his fair share of women in his life – women who were after him because of his looks or because they were interested in his money; every single one of them had slunk around after him until he'd finally looked their way. Intimate encounters had been hurried and one sided – them trying to please him to ensure his loyalty while he worked quickly to assuage his lust. Back then, all he'd wanted was his concentration – to assuage his cock so that he could work without distraction.

Being with Cecilia was a different experience entirely. Though he knew there was no way she could be a virgin, she had acted as if she'd never known a man's touch. Even the tiniest slide of his fingers between her legs had drawn whimpers of pleasure; she seemed, indeed, to be lost in it, unable to function under its intensity.

He was intoxicated.

He'd never encountered a woman who had begged him not with her words, but with every quivering inch of her body. He didn't have to pretend that she wanted only him – he knew it. It was evident in the way she looked at him, the way her lips parted when he entered her.

So, of course, there had been no only taking her once. He'd ended up coupling with her no less than three times, the third in the middle of the hall when she'd been attempting to leave his apartment. He knew it made him insufferable, but if she'd slapped him, told him off or threatened him, he would have let her go. It was obvious that there was something she was eager to get back to.

However, every time he touched her, she melted against him, raised her mouth for his kisses and let him carry her back to bed to ravish her again.

One time, he'd told himself.

Before he'd been so certain that a quick, mindless fuck would get her out of his system. Now, he was beginning to discover that with Cecilia Thompson, there could be no such thing. The question was: what to do about it? She was a good PA and he didn't want to lose her over something as trivial as his not being able to control his own desires.

But if the response of her body was any indication, she wouldn't mind any future advances.

Alexander's eyes fell on the Miller file, open on his desk. The case was set to go to court this Wednesday, and despite all the distraction he'd encountered, he still had a solid prosecution. That, he would have to admit, was thanks in part to Cecilia. Her digging up extra information to bolster his own had lent to one of the most convincing lines for conviction he'd ever come up with.

He would have to thank her.

And not by bending her over his desk.

Running a hand through his hair, he glanced at the clock again. Nine minutes past eight. If she didn't come in, what would he do then? Inevitably, he knew, his lust for her would cool. He'd forget the slide of her fragrant skin against his and push past her amazing work ethic.

He'd find someone else, and perhaps it would be for the better.

The thought made him scowl.

He didn't want anyone else. He wanted Cecilia; and if she didn't arrive in the next two minutes, he was going to be forced to hunt her down. He attempted to go through the Miller file for perhaps thirty seconds before casting it aside in frustration. He was on the cusp of calling Margaret when his intercom buzzed.

He picked it up on the first ring.

"Cecilia?"

"...no, sir." Margaret's careful soprano returned. "She's still not here. Should I call her?"

Alexander fumed silently. "No." He cut off the connection without another word. For the next half an hour, the man paced back and forth in his office, trying and failing to list all the state cases he'd worked on in the past year – backwards.

If she had been so disturbed by their evening together, why hadn't she said something? She had always been straight forward with him before. He crossed into his anteroom, splashing water on his face to try and cool his temper. Alexander found himself wondering if perhaps he had pushed her too far, too soon. She had been tipsy from the wine he'd bought, though not so much so that he thought her judgment severely impaired. She'd had any number of opportunities to tell him no...to change her mind...

But she'd chosen him – his bed and his demon lusts.

Close to nine o'clock, Alexander pulled on his coat and sauntered from his office, expression irate. When he stepped up to Margaret's desk, the young woman looked up at him, her eyes wide.

"Mr. Cross?"

"What address do we have on file for Cecilia?"

Margaret's fingers flew over the keyboard in search of the address and not two minutes later she had printed it on a notepad for him. No sooner was the piece of paper in his hand then he swept into the elevator, headed for the parking garage.

As he drove towards southern Brooklyn, he took several deep, calming breaths. Alexander could count on one hand the number of times he'd lost control of himself. This, he asserted, wasn't losing control. This was seeking answers. If Cecilia was going to hide from him, he was going to have to seek her out.

He pulled out of the Holland Tunnel and onto the streets of the lower borough, following his GPS directions carefully. The streets were still icy from the last snowfall, and even as incensed as he was, he wasn't about to do something so stupid as crashing his car. Greenpoint and Williamsburg were alive with pedestrians this early in the morning, and the neighborhoods around them teamed with people going about their daily business.

As he drove further into Brooklyn, however, newer, more posh apartment buildings grew fewer and fewer. Crowds thinned. Eventually, he began coming up on abandoned buildings, boarded up storefronts and questionable gangs in dark clothes on the street corners. Alexander frowned, checking his GPS. Was he going in the right direction?

According to the automated voice, he was. He was no more than two minutes from Cecilia's house.

He drove silently through the neighborhood, stopping at lights where he was sure drug deals were going on mere feet away, young men with shifty gazes glancing up and down streets to check for police activities.

These were the neighborhoods from which crime poured into the city. These were the places he was trying to change. He realized that he ventured into them so little that he couldn't possibly fathom if he was making a difference to any of these people. He went on statistics – and statistics called him the best thing to happen to the law in New York city in the past four decades.

But there were still slums, still street children.
Still addicts.

Through his tinted windows, Alexander watched a man light up on the street and his eyes narrowed, his fingers twitching on the steering wheel. It was times like this that he was tempted to do as his father urged him; to emerge from an unmarked car, fists flying, delivering justice to those who would pray on the innocent.

He remembered the blood that had spattered the kitchen floor, his mother's twitching fingers as his father had held her, the life ebbing from her body. He remembered seeing the hunched, pockmarked figure of her killer escaping through the same window he'd use to enter with a handful of her jewelery.

That man was being served three warm meals a day. He was given two hours of supervised exercise, and Alexander was paying for his every day expenses with his tax dollars.

Some men deserved to die....and lived anyway.

He pulled up short in front of the address Margaret had given him, peering up at the decrepit apartment building before him. For a moment, all he could do was stare. The building barely looked fit for human habitation. Cecilia came into work everyday on time, well-dressed and well-rested. This made to be a mistake. Margaret must have pulled the wrong address by mistake.

He opened the door, stepping from the Mercedes before closing and locking the door behind him. Then, slowly, he advanced on the front entryway of the building. He was wasting his time here. Most likely whoever was at *this* address would be too doped up to answer the door if he did ring the bell. He was going to have to chastise Margaret for sending him all the way out here for nothing.

He found apartment 1B with little difficulty. It was on the first floor at the corner and he grimaced as he stepped around a pile of garbage blocking the walkway. Where was sanitation in this part of the city? On perpetual holiday?

He was reaching down to depress the bell for the small, stained door before him when it opened.
From within the residence emerged a head of dark curls that had been spread across his pillow just the previous evening, and Alexander's breath caught in his throat.

Honey eyes met his and widened.

"Cross?"

She was clad as impeccably as always, in a linen skirt and button up shirt with her thin winter coat over her shoulder, her bag on one arm. For a moment, Alexander couldn't believe his eyes.

She lived *here*? In the heart of one of the poorest neighborhoods he'd visited in the city?

Cecilia was looking at him nervously as she closed the door behind herself. The glimpse he caught of the interior of the apartment was enough to make his chest seize – door-less cabinets, a battered refrigerator, and shedding furniture. "Mr. Cross...what are you doing here?"

"*This* is your apartment?" His inquiry escaped in a hard demand that made her take a step back. "You live *here*?"

For a moment, pain was evident in her large eyes before she seemed to steel herself, lifting her chin as she faced him. "Does it matter? What are you *doing* all the way out here?"

"You're over an *hour* late for work," he returned curtly, his chest tight. This was what she was in such a rush to return to every evening? This was what she'd wanted to leave him for last night? The woman worked eight, sometimes nine hour shifts doing impossible tasks and didn't even have proper human amenities? "Why?"

"Quiet!" She suddenly looked around, her expression wary as she spoke to him. When her eyes finally met his again, they had acquired their own spark of irritation. "I had some personal issues. I was going to call, but things got...busy."

"Busy? At eight in the morning?" A harsh bark of laughter escaped him. "I thought we agreed to be adults about this."

Her eyes widened and her mouth dropped open as she stared up at him in disbelief. "You think this is about last night?"

"Isn't it?"

He could probably be heard down the block, but he was far from caring. He'd get his answers from her before he left – *all* of them. The two of them glared hotly at one another for a moment, until the creaking of the thin door caught their attentions.

Alexander swung his head around to see a thin brown face edging from the doorway.

It was a boy.

A very sick boy. His skin was pale and sweat marred his brow, his mouth a grimace of pain. Even that, however, couldn't take away the sharp resemblance in the child's features. The district attorney watched, shocked, as Cecelia wheeled around, her expression alarmed. "Xaviar?" Her voice softened decibels from the tone she'd used just seconds earlier as she swung the door open. "Honey, get back in bed. It's freezing." She immediately wrapped an arm around the youth – who appeared in his early teens – and led him back inside.

Alexander stood outside the cracked door, his eyes wide, as bits of dialogue reached his ears.

"Who's that?" The boy's voice was low and husky with fever.

"Just one of my work friends. Don't worry."

"A *loud* work friend."

"Xaviar Thompson, you get your sick behind back to bed! I'm going to get your medicine and I'll be back in ten minutes."

"Are you going to work?"

"*Bed.*"

For moments, there was silence. Then, the door swung open once more and Cecilia reappeared, her expression grim. Without a word, she shut the door behind her and locked it, before turning back to Alexander.

"You have a son." The words fell from his mouth in low disbelief and she merely glared at him before crunching down the walk and past him, headed towards her car. It took Alexander a moment to find his feet, but when he did, he strode after her, a hundred questions streaking through his head. Until this exact moment, Cecelia Thompson had merely been a woman who haunted his carnal thoughts.

She was a fantastic PA and a dedicated worker, but he'd come here convinced that she was shamed by what had happened between them; shamed enough to hide from him.

He'd thought of her as a purely sexual creature.

She was, he was only beginning to realize, an enormous amount more than that. "Cecilia, wait." He caught her arm halfway down the walk, pulling her around to face him. Before a single word could leave his mouth, however, she beat him to the punch.

"He's not my son, he's my brother; though he might as well be my child. I'm his only parent. I came home last night to find he'd eaten some bad food from our shitty fridge because *I* wasn't home to make dinner. His stomach is messed up and I *need* to get him some medicine. Pardon me for not taking a breather from all the *puke* this morning to call in. I figured I'd just wait for you to yell at me later, but it appears you've brought the party to me." She yanked her arm from his grip. "So, am I fired?"

For a moment, he just stared at her, utterly at a loss for words.

Only parent? To a teenage boy? In *this* dump?

"Can't you afford a better apartment on what I'm paying you?"

Cecilia groaned, turning from him to start for her car again, her face flaming. "We're not talking about this. You're not even supposed to *be* here."

Before she could even slip the keys into the lock, Alexander caught her shoulder and whipped her around again, trapping her against the side of the vehicle with his body. His narrow green gaze demanded an answer. "Answer me. Can you or can't you afford something better than this cesspool?"

"This 'cesspool' is all we have!" She shot back at him, her eyes burning in a mixture of embarrassment and rage. "In case you haven't noticed, Cross, the economy's not really booming right now. I haven't had a job in almost a year. I'm just getting back on my feet and it's going to take a while for me to climb back out of the hole I've dug us into. Do you want me to call you my savior? Fine. You're my savior. Should I beg for my job? Or was that already forfeit when I let you fuck me?"

"*Quiet.*"

His voice cracked through the cold air like a whip, making the woman before him jump despite the intensity of her tirade. She immediately fell silent, leaning back against the car as her chest rose and fell rapidly.

Christ, she was like a lioness protecting her cub.

How had this escaped his attention? He'd hired the woman without even glancing at her background. Of course, he'd had other things on his mind at the time, but this? This was deplorable. She drove downtown everyday to work in his plush office and had to return home to drafty walls and doors that wouldn't withstand a strong kicking?

He'd been so taken with her, so blinded by raw desire that he hadn't done even the smallest shred of homework on her. Certainly, he knew her social security number and that she paid her taxes, but this?

He'd been the one to keep her late the previous evening. He'd been the one that had kept her from her brother. Him and his obsessive lust.

"Come with me."

Taking her hand in a firm grip, he pulled her away from her car and across the street to where his was parked. "Cross, no. I can't go to work right now. I have to-"

"If you don't want to lose your job, get in the car now." Her eyes widened in shock before she glared at him, the beginnings of hatred in her honey gaze. She slid into the car stiffly and he joined her in seconds. A minute after he started the car, he was off and back around the corner.

He remembered seeing a drugstore three lights down and, sure enough, he found it. Without a word, he pulled up into the parking lot and stepped from the car. "Stay here." Before Cecilia could protest, he'd locked her into the car and was striding toward the shabby establishment.

He bought three bottles of Pepto Bismol, some Tums, a few liter bottles of ginger ale, several cans of soup and a loaf of white bread. The cashier stared at him in disbelief as he passed him a hundred dollar bill, but quickly made change beneath Alexander's intimidating glower.

Upon returning to the car, he set his loot at Cecelia's feet before finally meeting her bewildered gaze. "There. That should last you until he's well."

She looked from him to the bags and then back again. Slowly, she began to shake her head. "No. I can't take this."

He cursed lowly, his fingers curling into the steering wheel tightly. "Why not?"

"I'm not some charity case. I work for you. You pay me – unless you're firing me, I don't need-"

"For the love of *God*, woman, I am not firing you!" He burst. "And this isn't about charity. It's about getting your brother the medicine he needs so *you* can get back to your place in the office. You're going to take the meds – end of story."

With that, he reversed out of the drugstore and made the quick drive back to her apartment building. By now there was a group of young men on the corner, watching his car with no small amount of interest. Alexander frowned at them, reaching over to push the door open for her. "Go. I'll wait for you."

This time, when Cecilia looked at him, her gaze was unsure. Hesitantly, she leaned forward to pick up the bags before exiting the car, hurrying back toward her apartment. Alexander watched her, his mind working overtime to process the information he'd learned.

This woman was one of the most hardworking he'd ever met. She'd been jobless for God knew how long and worked long days under the pressure of his scrutiny to come home to a rat hole and a brother sick from what was probably a toxic refrigerator.

And he'd seduced her.

Groaning, Alexander drew his hands over his face in frustration.

He was a monster.

"Thank you."

Looking up from where he'd been working on a new case file, the district attorney found his PA standing in the door of his office. Since he'd driven her to work the previous day, there had been precious little talk between them. He'd given her her tasks, valiantly staving off his still rampant hunger for her, and attempted to bury himself in his work.

To forget what he'd seen.

Cecilia obviously wanted to keep her private life exactly that – private; and by seeking her out, he'd crossed a boundary.

He seemed to be pressing his luck with this woman – first with her body and then with her secrets.

But now, here she was; expression humble, stance respectful, as she looked at him over his desk. He straightened as she continued. "For the medicine, I mean. Xaviar's already feeling a whole lot better."

"Good." He nodded, managing to keep his eyes from roving to where her bosom stretched the front of the cream-colored sweater she wore. Christ, he was such an animal. Even after seeing the squalor in which she lived and knowing how much trouble he caused her, he still ached for her. She continued to invade his thoughts and frustrate his work. "Was there anything else?"

"Yes!" Her answer was a bit too forceful as she hurried forward to place several files on his desk. "I've typed up Tyler Baldwell's statement. Also Stevens', though there's room for revision if you want to include more. Also, your cleaners called to say your suit is ready and I've cleared your schedule for the charity event this Thursday."

He took the paperwork from her, electricity tingling in his fingertips when they brushed hers.

Damn. The charity. He'd almost completely forgotten in the upset of the previous day.

Cecilia turned to leave his office, only to pause with one foot out the door. In a split second, she returned to his side before leaning down to press her mouth to his.

For a moment, Alexander was taken by surprise – but only a moment.

His fingers rose to tangle in her hair as he pulled her into his lap and flush against his body.

Yes. This was what he'd wanted for the past forty-eight hours. What he'd ached for even as he'd watched her chatting idly with Margaret or taking messages on the phone. Her mouth burned against his and her tongue was like silk – driving him out of his mind.

But *this* was wrong. He'd already overstepped his boundaries twice. To do it again would be unwise. Even if Cecilia did want him as desperately as he wanted her, he couldn't use her while it was convenient to him with the knowledge of what she returned to every evening after serving his every whim.

He wasn't that cold-hearted.

What she needed was an escape -and perhaps, in doing so, she could take pressure from him as well.

Almost painfully, he broke the kiss to cup her chin, lifting her gorgeous face so he could take in the sight of her swollen lips and desirous, hooded eyes. He could take her right here, *right* now if he so chose.

"Take the rest of the afternoon off." Her eyelids fluttered as the lusty haze left them and her eyes widened.

"Excuse me?"

But he was already rising from his chair and reaching for his coat. "We're taking the rest of the afternoon off. Tell Margaret she's in charge."

Cecilia's face flamed. "*Cross*, you can't be serious! It's the middle of the day-" She gasped as he hedged her between the desk and his immense body, his thumb brushing over the softness of her cheek as he smirked in amusement.

"It's not for what you think, Cecilia. Though I hate to disappoint." With that statement, he released her, striding from his office and leaving her to hurry after him in his wake. She barely had a moment to speak to Margaret before sliding into the elevator right before it shut. "Where are we going?" Her tone was breathless from the pace he'd set.

Alexander's lips quirked.

She'd see.

Getting Cecilia into the shop he'd chosen was a trial in and of itself. When he'd parked on the corner of Fifth Avenue, he knew she suspected something. Now, standing in the middle of

Saks, she appeared like a deer in headlights.

"Oh my God, what are we doing here?"

The only thing that kept her from bolting was his firm grip on her arm. "Shopping." He gestured to a nearby saleswoman, who was only too happy to glide over to them with a wide smile on her face.

"Welcome to Saks Mr. Cross. How may I help you today?"

"We need to see a few formal gowns. Size...eight perhaps?" He gave Cecilia a once over that was hardly needed. Since having her, every detail of her size was etched firmly into his mind. "I think lighter colors would be best. Something that stands out."

"Of course, sir. Would you like tea and cookies while I pull some items for you?"

At that exact moment, Cecilia's stomach growled loudly, the sound permeating the store. When he raised a brow at the woman, she adopted a sheepish expression, refusing to meet his gaze. "I'll take that as a yes." The saleswoman grinned at them both before breezing off in her efficient manner.

Almost immediately, Cecilia turned to him, her eyes wide. "Formal gowns? What are you talking about? I can't afford anything in here!"

"You'll need a gown for the charity ball Thursday," He replied smoothly. "You're going to be my plus one."

"Your-what?"

"I'll need you by my side on Thursday night. Consider it a work function."

Cecilia was gaping at him in a way that he honestly found very endearing. Alexander had found many women alluring in his life but he couldn't remember the last time he'd actually found one cute.

"Here's your tea District Attorney Cross." Another smiling attendant had arrived with a tray that consisted of an elegant china pot, two teacups and a three tiered tray of pastries from the store's world renowned bakery. The moment Cecilia's eyes lit on the cakes, they darkened in hunger.

Alexander now realized how frequently he'd seen the expression on her face – not for sex, but for proper food.

How much was she eating?

The attendant sat the tray down on a low table in the waiting area before leaving them to it. Even so, Cecilia only stared at it for a moment, unmoving. Alexander arched a brow. "When was the last time you had a proper meal? One you *didn't* feed to your brother?" Her cheeks flushed as she gazed at him embarrassed. He sighed, taking her hand in a gentle yet firm grip to lead her around the table to sit upon the chaise beside it. "Eat, Cecilia."

Still, she hesitated. "Cross, I-"

"You're going to consume this entire tray. Every last crumb. And then we're going to find you a dress for the charity ball. If you utter one more protest I will drag you back to the car and have my way with you in the middle of Fifth Avenue for all to see. Do you understand me?"

A flash of hunger touched wide eyes and for a moment, Alexander knew she was considering rebellion, of only for the promise of sexual deviancy. But after a moment, she merely lowered her gaze and lifted a petite four from the tray to take a bite. The expression on her face was well worth the fuss she'd put up leaving the office.

As the attended headed their way with a number of designer gowns draped over her arm, he allowed himself a small smile.

He was beginning to discover exactly what it was that made Cecilia Thompson tick.

**

He hated his school.

Staring down the hall as he shut his locker, Xaviar shook his head. Some girl was scrapping with her one-time friend, ripping out her weave as she insulted her at the top of her voice.

There was a boy who should probably be halfway though college swinging his weight around, bullying freshman and trying to look up girls skirts. The smell of weed was rampant in the bathrooms of both sexes and most of the students had no interest whatsoever in the material desperate teachers tried to instill in them.

One more year.

One more year of this and he could go back to Harlem and his Magnet school – Cece had promised.

At the memory, the young man frowned.

His sister worked so hard. She thought she could hide it from him – the way she pinched pennies to send him on school trips and worried over finances; how she gave him an extra plate at dinner and went hungry herself to make sure he had enough to eat.

Many of his peers had siblings that they constantly scrapped with, but Xaviar was no fool. His sister was utterly and totally devoted to him, and all he wanted to do was make her proud. He was too young to remember his father, but the look on Cece's face on the rare times he asked about him was enough.

The man was a criminal – the lowest of the low. To be anything like him would mean breaking his sister's heart; so Xaviar did well in school. He got top mark and worked hard towards his goal of being an engineer.

However, the one thing that got to him was how little he could contribute to his small family. Though Cece had gotten a new job and things were looking up for them, money was still tight. If only there was some way he could get a job and boost their income the tiniest bit...he knew it would make his sister happy.

"'ey, Xaviar!"

He was jerked from his thoughts by the call of one of his few friends, Malcolm, shortly after exiting the school building. His lips curving into a grin, he advanced on his friend to award him a fist bump before hoisting his heavy book bag higher on his shoulders. "Hey man. What's up?"

"Aw, nothin much. Same ole, same ole." Though he could

Righting Wrongs

consider the older boy his friend, Xaviar knew that Malcom didn't have the same regard for learning that he did. In short, he was lazy, and wasn't beyond doing the random odd job for some of the more dangerous members of the community when he was feeling bored. "Heard that fine sister of yours got visited by a white boy the other day."

Xaviar grimaced at the thought of anyone calling his sister 'fine'. "It was her boss. He was mad at her for being late to work."

"And he came all the way out to the ghetto? Thas cold! She get fired, man?"

Xaviar shook his head. Thank God for small favors. "*Thas* good man. *Thas* cool she dodged the bullet on that one. I know ya'll hurtin."

Xaviar scowled. Shooting shit was one thing, but he didn't want to talk about his family's financial situation. It was always a sore subject. "Hey, Xav, man, I wanna help you out. I know some guys that need a little runnin' done. They pay well."

Xaviar's frown deepened.

"Running" was street talk for carrying drugs over enemy turfs to other dealers. While the job was supposed to be relatively easy and safe for the runners themselves, what they carried was more than enough to put him off.

Heroin, crack, cocaine...he didn't want any of that stuff near him. That was what had turned his father into the monster he was and landed him in jail – probably for the rest of his life. "Nah, man." He waved Malcolm off in what he hoped was a casual manner. "I'm not into that type of thing."

"Even if they're running a hundred, two hundred a trip?"

Despite his staunch attitude towards drugs, the figure gave Xaviar pause.

Two hundred dollars was a lot of money. That was groceries or gas for a week – money that Cece wouldn't have to bow and scrape for.

But still...running was no joke. He'd never even stepped foot into that world before, and he had no desire to be eaten alive. "Nah. I can't be nobody's fool. Those big dogs are crazy." He turned, preparing to head down the front steps of the school when Malcolm spoke again.

"Big dogs, huh? Well, what about me, homes? I'm a little fish, we tight, and I just so *happen*," He flashed a small plastic baggie from his pocket and Xaviar's eyes widened at the finely milled white powder within, "to have a little bit of product I'd like to get over to Vic on twenty sixth. Five blocks."

Xaviar just stared at his friend. He had no idea how Malcom had gotten his hands on drugs or who he'd gotten them from; the boy was a petty thief, sure, but he wasn't big time. He wasn't bright enough.

Running for him wouldn't be too bad…it wouldn't be as if he was *doing* the drugs after all. Only carrying them. And after he dropped them off, that would be two hundred dollars in his pocket! Two hundred that he could give to his sister!

He found himself actually considering the job.

It would help Cece out a lot, and he hated to see her struggling to make ends meet for him.

"Do we have a deal?" Now Malcolm held out the tiny white bag, its contents glinting in the sun.

For a moment, Xaviar stared at it.

He reached out, and his fingers closed around the product.

CHAPTER 6 - CHANGE

Three months later

"I've reformed, your honor. What I did...it was at a bad point in my life. I had a momentary lapse in sanity."

Cece fought, hard, against rolling her eyes in full view of the judge. She'd risen at five o'clock this morning to search out their defendant and drag him into court at Alexander's instructions. No small feat when the man had kept her up most of the night before putting her through her paces. At the memory of his hands roving her skin, she suppressed a shudder, trying to focus on the case.

She had no idea how he did it.

For the past three months, she'd watched Alexander with growing awe. It was one thing to hear about the man and his dedication to the city, and quite another to watch the way with which he tore through the urban underbelly, cutting hard and cutting deep. While, in the first few weeks of her employment, she'd been so wrapped up in learning the ropes that she hadn't spent more than an hour or two in the courtroom, now things were completely different.

Cece watched Mario Tellson on the stand – a squat, burly man with a broken face. He was charged with five counts of rape and a few more of domestic abuse. The man was a known member of the Russian mafia and one of the most prominent figures in the Manhattan underworld. Alexander had been after him for years, hoping that a successful prosecution would open doors previously closed to him.

The lawyer defending Tellson was an old rival of Alexander's, and the animosity between the two men was evident in the tense atmosphere in the courtroom. When Cece's eyes fell on the district attorney seated at the table before the judge, her heart stuttered slightly in her stomach.

He never failed to take her breath away.

The man was clad in a starched gray suit with a dark tie that hugged his tall form. His blonde hair was slicked back from his face and his face shaved absolutely clean. The image he projected was absolutely no nonsense, his piercing green eyes riveted on the man on the stand. It had taken her a few weeks of watching him in the courtroom, but Cece had taught herself to read the emotions that the man prided himself on hiding.

He was pissed.

Beyond pissed.

Alexander had been chasing Tellson for a good half of his career and now the man was trying to wiggle out of his conviction. She knew he wouldn't stand for it.

He never did.

If there was one thing she'd learned about Alexander in the past few months, it was how he ruled the courtroom. It didn't matter if the man came in defending or prosecuting, he ruled the courthouse with an unmistakable air of power that served to shake his opponents to the core. They knew his reputation – knew that he couldn't be bribed or bought off – and it made him all the more dangerous.

Though Cece had never been terribly interested in law, she couldn't help but watch him now, utterly transfixed.

"What my client is trying to say, your honor, is that the mafia influenced his way of thinking. He worked for them only to protect his own life." Owen Pentsworth was a thin, vile man with a thick mustache and absolutely no moral character. He worked for whoever paid him the most, be it honest men or criminals.

Criminals were usually richer.

Alexander absolutely despised him – and the sentiment was rich in the way he glared at the man.

"Objection, your honor." Cross' voice was curt and sharp, ringing through the courtroom with authority. "Leading the witness."

"Sustained." The wizened judge Carlisle glanced at Pentworth with barely contained disdain. "I'm sure Mr. Tenson can lie for himself, Pentworth."

The case didn't last for very long.

They had been in court for three days as it was – three days of Tenson trying to dodge the inevitable, and it seemed like Alexander was ready to bring the matter to an end.

The conclusion was brutal. Within thirty minutes, the district attorney had gotten the judge to increase the severity of Tellson's sentence from ten to fifteen years in jail; his prosecution was so scathing that by the time court adjourned for the jury to deliberate, Pentworth was shaking in anger and Tellson was white with fear.

Cece waited for Alexander outside the courtroom, as she usually did, rendered breathless by his brutality.

He was absolutely, completely ruthless – but then again, that was what Manhattan's criminal underworld required.

As he came up beside her, she handed him his briefcase without a word. It wasn't until were descending the front steps of the courthouse that the man spoke. "The jury will be unanimous. It's a pity he can't do life."

"Well, it's a bit hard to prove the man did more than just what we got him on." Cece's reply was apologetic. "If I'd had more time, I could have dug up more -"

"No. You did well. As always."

She flushed at the praise. Despite the fact that she'd been working as the man's PA for close to five months now, she knew that he didn't award it lightly. What happened in the courtroom and what happened...*between* them were two completely separate things.

But she had to say...the latter relationship had changed immensely since she'd first agreed to celebratory French with the man.

At the time, Cece had believed herself capable of only one evening of pleasure with Alexander Cross. After all, she'd wanted the man since she'd first laid eyes on him. A part of her – admittedly, a part drunk on half a bottle of wine – had been convinced that the best course of action would be to get him out of her system.

But things hadn't gone quite as she'd hoped they would.

Not only had once not been enough with Cross, but even three times had still left her craving. To be honest, if she had the man every night, it probably still wouldn't be enough. He'd awakened something wild in her – something primal that she thought she'd seen the last of a long time ago.

And that wasn't all.

The morning after what she'd thought might have been her first and last mistake working with Cross, he'd come to her house when she'd been late for work. Xaviar had been violently ill – something she'd had to see to before she could think of stepping foot outside the door. Of course, Cross venturing into her neighborhood had exposed things that she would rather have kept secret: her sub-par living conditions, the difficulties of the past year, and also the very existence of her brother himself.

She hadn't wanted her home life to spill over into her place of employment.

But Alexander had blown all that out of the water.

Surprisingly, he hadn't judged her for being surrogate single mother to a teenager. Instead, he'd forced her to take the medicine and supplies he'd bought for Xaviar before giving her a ride back to work – refusing to fire her.

Things had only gotten...weirder from there.

Cece had told herself numerous times that she'd been lucky to get this job; that out of desperation she'd taken something outside of the fashion field to provide for her brother and dig them out of the ditch of poverty the economy had driven them into. She would save, she'd promised herself; save until things could get better. It was important to get Xaviar into a better school and to move out of south Brooklyn

However, Alexander was turning her plans of hard work and dedication somewhat on their head. It wasn't that the man wasn't hard on her – he still expected her to perform above and beyond his expectations and operate as the glue that kept his office together. That hadn't changed. What *had* changed, however, was how he expected her to do those things while he completely altered every notion she'd had about what men were supposed to do for women.

She'd fought him at first.

The medicine had been hard to accept, because she'd always been independent; but it had been for Xaviar's health so she'd swallowed her pride. The dress had come harder.

As she slid into the passenger seat of Alexander's Mercedes, she frowned, remembering the obscene amount of money he'd dropped on an Alexander McQueen gown for her to wear to accompany him to a benefit he hadn't even wanted to go to. Though she'd told herself she'd stuff the thing in the back of her own closet and wear a less gaudy dress, the garment was so damn beautiful she'd been tempted into it on the night of the ball.

A confection of turquoise and blue silk that had felt like heaven against her skin...even now, three months after the fact, she still pulled it out to run her fingers across the fabric in awe. But the dress had only been the beginning of a multitude of gifts that Alexander had bestowed upon her. In the guise of it being for work, the man had bought her a new laptop – one that she could take with her wherever she pleased. Then he'd brought space heaters for every room in her house, citing that if her fingers were too cold to type, how could she used the damned thing at home.

Righting Wrongs

He probably suspected that she cut back on her own diet to make sure that Xaviar got enough, so he'd resorted to stuffing her face with take out at work. She'd completely given up refusing him after the first few weeks as the man would find ways to *make* her eat – some of them embarrassing. Then, there were the other gifts: a DKNY watch to make sure she was always on time (she'd only been late once), a gorgeous leather briefcase to hold her paperwork (of which, he insisted, she had copious amounts), and not one, but *two* new coats – each one three times as thick as her threadbare go-to and lusciously warm. The man insisted that she needed proper court wear, but by now, Cece knew that he merely gained some kind of sadistic satisfaction watching her become flustered by his gifts.

He was her boss, and she knew that this went far beyond the realm of what an employer should do for an employee.

Of course, the fact that they were sleeping together was another factor to add to the confusing mix.

To be honest, Cece had thought the man would be bored of her quite early. The fact that he'd assumed that she'd flee from him after their first encounter attested to the fact. However, he seemed to have a hunger for her that never waned. After the charity ball, he'd invited her back to his apartment for a drink – to "clear their heads".

Cece had known very well what he wanted; and even though she'd told herself she wouldn't give into the man again, no matter what kindnesses he'd paid her, she'd tumbled into his bed for the second time very sober and almost weak with desire for him.

She hadn't been able to resist him since.

It was a strange balance they maintained. In the office, Cross was never anything but completely professional. He delegated certain duties to her, which she did without question, knowing how important her work was to maintaining his hold on the city's crime rate.

However, after hours...everything was different.

The man took her to dinner – to authentic French, Italian, African fusion and everything in between. When she mentioned that she'd never been to an Opera, he'd took her, despite the fact that she doubted that the man himself truly enjoyed the show. He constantly asked about her and Xaviar, and even though Cece had tried as best she could to keep from speaking with him about matters that made her uncomfortable, she soon found herself voicing her fears about her younger brother's education and the environment in which he was forced to go to school.

She couldn't help it. Alexander had coaxed the admission from her in his typical way – brusque demand followed by sweet seduction. The man seemed, somehow, to take an interest in her in a way most men never had. He asked her about her prior career, her relationship with her coworkers, and her family.

The last subject, however, was one that she kept completely mum. She'd never been comfortable discussing her parents with anyone, and as long as she lived, she didn't think things would change. So far as she was concerned, it was just her and Xaviar against the world – and that was perfectly fine with her.

"It's nearly four." She jerked back to the present to take in the man addressing her, swallowing thickly at the striking figure poured into a suit at her side. "Shall we finish early for the day and get dinner?" The request was innocent enough, but Cece knew full well that Alexander would want her to return to his place after wards.

Righting Wrongs

The prospect of the man mouth and hands on her in places that had haunted her dreams was almost enough to undo her, but she knew that she couldn't.

Not tonight.

She'd been spending precious little time with Xaviar as it was, and tonight, she'd promised that she'd help him with his science project. It wasn't that she was a terribly adept scientist, only that she wanted to do whatever she could for the boy. This was merely an excuse to dote on him.

"I promised Xaviar I would help him with his homework tonight." She shot Alexander a small smile, knowing that the excuse was one of the only he accepted for not having her in his arms. As it was, Xaviar wasn't very clear on what was happening between them. He probably thought she worked late and had pulled a few all nighters, slaving for her boss. God knew she didn't strut around displaying her intimate affairs so brazenly before the impressionable teen. The last time he'd seen Alexander, she and he had been having a shouting match on her front doorstep.

She didn't think her brother's opinion of the district attorney was the best. However, if things continued the way they were for much longer, she wasn't going to be able to avoid properly introducing them. Xaviar deserved to meet the man who demanded so much of her time, and she supposed that if she was going to be so secretive with certain aspects of her life, there were some she could allow Alexander a brief glimpse into.

"I see." Alexander took the turn onto Fifth Avenue, headed uptown. For a moment, there was comfortable silence between them, before the man's low baritone colored the air again. "How about we get a pizza and head to your place then?"

Cece tensed slightly.

In the three months they'd been engaged in...whatever it was between them, Alexander had respected her boundaries. After the first time he'd sought her out, he hadn't returned to her house, knowing that it was a source of tension for her. Now, three months later, here he was asking to go the one place he knew she was sensitive about.

Asking was the key word.

Alexander was her boss. If he wanted something from her, he could demand it; in fact, he often used such power to his advantage – both in and out of the bedroom. However, in this instance, he knew better than to offend her in such a way. His tone was soft, inquiring.

He wanted her permission.

For a moment, Cece bit her lip in contemplation. Xaviar wouldn't be prepared to meet him tonight; he was just expecting his sister home. However...pizza did sound good. She supposed it couldn't do *too* much damage to have Alexander downstairs while she helped her brother. She was sure he'd understand the need for family time.

Then, the only matter left was her embarrassment over the state of her living space. Even in the cold early spring, there were roaches, termites and mice. Though the house was now warm - thanks to the heaters Alexander had bought – there were some things that just couldn't be fixed.

"My place isn't..." She struggled to find the right words, staring out the window at passing cars with a frown. "It isn't anywhere near as nice as yours."

Righting Wrongs

Alexander snorted, glancing over at her. "I daresay you're a better decorator than I. I'm sure it's lovely."

If it were any other man, Cecilia would be certain, utterly *certain* that she was being mocked. But Alexander had already seen what she had to offer. He knew how sensitive she was about her financial situation. Hell, he'd offered to front her a portion of her salary that would have gotten her out of South Brooklyn in half the time she'd planned – but she'd refused. She'd make it in time, on her own.

Taking a deep breath, she nodded slowly. "Ok...Pizza sounds good."

Despite the tantalizing smell of the sausage and onion pizza, Cece was nervous the entire way to her apartment. Would Xaviar and Alexander get along? God knew both of them could be stubborn when they put their minds to it. They were the men who currently ruled her life...and it would be a Godsend if they weren't at one anothers throats.

While Cross saw to the pizza, Cece let herself into the house first. Xaviar was sitting on the couch, obviously waiting for her. He bounced to his feet when he saw her with a huge grin. "Hey, Cece! Did you have a good day at work?"

It was nice to see him so enthusiastic. Usually the young man was buried in homework when she got home, too absorbed to spare her more than a quick hello.

"It was pretty good." She returned his infectious grin with one of her own. "Big court case. We've got it in the bag."

"Great. Listen, I've got a surprise."

Ah, so that was what this was all about? She wondered what it was. It was still ages until her birthday. Whenever Xaviar worked himself up into surprising her, she knew it was important to him. Dropping her bag on the coffee table, Cece closed her eyes with great ceremony. "Ok, tell me when."

Xaviar laughed lowly, she sound making her heart light. "Hold out your hand."

She did so, lifting the palm upward.

Immediately, several pieces of crumpled paper she recognized as bills were placed into her hand and Cecilia's eyes popped open. Lying in her palm were a few crushed tens. She raised her eyes to see her brother looking up at her eagerly. "I started selling candy with my allowance, so I could help out. It's for you."

She felt her heart twist in her chest as her throat grew tight.

Xaviar had tried to raise money.

For *her*.

She tried to keep her every day struggles from him – to make sure he got enough to eat and plenty of rest – but it seemed as if her troubles were still transparent. She took a deep breath, closing her hand around the bills.

She knew better than to refuse them. That would hurt the teenager's pride. Instead, she would stash them in a drawer somewhere to return to him on his birthday or some other pertinent occasion. The young woman blinked back tears as her smile widened. "Thanks, Xaviar. I really appreciate it."

The young man beamed up at her proudly -

Righting Wrongs

At least until the door opened behind them to reveal Alexander toting a Benny's pizza box. When he saw the immense man, Xaviar's face fell. "What's he doing here?"

Immediately, Cece felt her heart sink. So the vibes she'd been getting from her younger brother hadn't been wrong. He wasn't too fond of Alexander.

Cross looked up at Xaviar's inquiry before arching a brow in her direction. The dark-haired woman steeled herself, practicing diplomacy. "Xaviar, you've met my boss, Mr. Cross?"

"Right." The teenager's eyes narrowed. "The guy who yelled at you in front of the house."

Cece suppressed a groan. "The man who's helping us get back on our feet?" Xaviar still remained on his guard, sizing up the man before him. In Cece's experience, most people who weren't familiar with Alexander tended to cower in fear at the sheer size of him. Xaviar stood straight and tall, his hazel eyes roving the man from head to foot. "What cha got there?"

The district attorney flipped open the box in his hand, exposing the extra large sausage and onion pizza. Cece knew that it was one of Xaviar's favorites. "Extra cheese, extra sausage." The man;s voice boomed through the small apartment. "Your sister thought you'd be hungry. I'm just going to wait until you guys are done working on your project so I can go over a few things with her...if that's alright with you."

Cece could only wait with bated breath. Alexander had made a big move – stepping off his quite lofty horse in order to extend a peace offering to the boy. Now, Xaviar simply had to decide to accept or scorn it. As she watched, the teenager reached into the box to withdraw a slice. He took a large bite, swallowed, and then took another. Finally, he gave Alexander a last once over. "Yeah, I guess that's cool."

Relief washed over her. Thank God for small favors.

Turning, Cece quickly turned to place the bills Xaviar had given her in the drawer of the coffee table before moving to take the pizza box from Alexander. The man caught her eye with a wry smirk as she moved to fix her own plate before placing his briefcase on the table. When he hunkered down on the couch, he made the ancient piece of furniture seem tiny, and she had to tear her eyes from him to hurry upstairs after Xaviar.

"Do you like this guy?"

Both of them were bent over the teen's biology book when he next spoke. His inquiry had Cece flushing crimson. Christ, she hoped it wasn't that obvious.

"Well..." She managed, trying to remember her diplomacy. "He's pretty nice. He hired me when I needed a job."

"Yeah, but that doesn't mean you *owe* him anything." Xaviar cut his eyes at her as he pulled out his paperwork. "You're already his slave all day at the office."

The dark-haired woman couldn't suppress a low laugh. If only Xaviar knew how right he was. Alexander Cross was nothing *less* than a slave driver – it hadn't taken her, or anyone else who worked in the office, long to learn that.

"That's true. But Mr. Cross is working for the good of the city. To try and make neighborhoods like ours safer." She reached out to touch her brother's shoulder gently. "I think it's worth a few hours of my time to help him."

Xaviar glanced up from his book with a mischievous smile. "As long as he's paying you."

Cece only rolled her eyes, pointing at a segment of text. "Alright, nosy. That's enough questions. Eat your pizza and lets work on this thing."

**

He hated to think of her here.

Ever since he'd learned exactly what kind of home Cecilia returned to every evening, Alexander had to resist the urge to interfere. The heaters had been something that had haunted him for weeks until he'd gotten her to accept them. This place...he had half a mind to find the landlord and prosecute him. Everything was broken – the lights flickered and the fridge leaked.

If he didn't know that Cecilia would resent him for it, he'd force her out of the place. Contrive some reason that she had to move so he could sleep better at night knowing that she didn't have to be in such a dump.

Over the past few months, he'd pondered several times: why did he care so goddamn much? The woman was his PA. Certainly, they'd become intimately involved. If anything, she was on his mind even more now that he could have her body at his leisure – but there was something far more than simple sexual attraction that fueled this...urge.

To protect. To provide.

Cristina Grenier

He must be losing his mind.

He'd barely known the woman a handful of weeks, and already he'd gone from lusting after her to picturing how he could change her life if she'd just let him. But Cece, he'd found, was more stubborn than any woman he'd ever known.

In Alexander's experience, women wanted attention lavished on them. They wanted gifts, praise and adulation. Cece only wanted these things if she truly deserved them, and even then, she was reluctant to accept them – at best. She'd nearly bitten his head off when he'd bought her gown for the charity ball.

She adored the dress. He could see the way her eyes lit when she put it on – but even so, she fought him. Here was a woman convinced that nice things could only be hers if she worked for them herself.

In that way, she was a lot like himself.

He had never found himself wanting to buy women gifts – to surprise the with things they'd only dreamed of, or craving their smile at the start of his day.

But she...she was different.

And so, Alexander knew that he was in very real trouble. So far, said trouble hadn't interceded on the work he did with the city. Cece's work as a PA, if anything, only helped him to be better at his job. If he ever slipped, it was from his own lack of attention – from distraction whenever the scent of her wafted over him as she brought him his morning coffee.

She was his...and yet there were so many ways she wasn't.

Righting Wrongs

If he was honest with himself, Alexander would have to admit that Cecilia was very private. She hardly ever spoke about her family or her past beyond the hardships she'd endured lately. When she was with him, it seemed that she was absorbed in he alone; and while he appreciated the sentiment immensely, he was left curious about what had molded her into the woman she was.

Strong, hard-working and steadfast...with a hint of vulnerability she struggled to hide from everyone she knew. Even Margaret, arguably the woman's closest friend in the office, had no clue about anything relating to Cecilia's past or her home life. His PA was careful, *very* careful, not to entangle her professional life with her personal life.

At least, she had been before *they* had happened.

Now that he was in her home, Alexander couldn't help but to move through the rooms on the first floor, listening to the steady hum of his lover working with her brother above him.

The walls were threadbare – there hadn't been much done in the way of decoration, but what wouldn't have ruined the walls further than they already were. Frowning, Alexander noticed a relative lack of family photos. In his own home, one couldn't turn a corner without running into some memory from his adolescence or childhood. Here, it seemed almost as if any traces of Cecilia's childhood had been erased in their entirety.

He paused in front of the kitchen, lifting a single framed image to look over. In the picture, there were three people: A dark-skinned man in a polo shirt and jeans with a pock-marked face, a girl that looked no older than eighteen with a mess of tameable hair in overalls, and the baby she was holding – a pale infant that didn't look more than a few days old.

For a moment, Alexander just stared. No doubt this was Cecilia's family. However, the distance between those in the picture was evident in the way they carried themselves. The pride that usually graced parents eyes in the presence of their children was no where in this man's. Young Cecilia looked awkward and out of place, and clutched the baby to her chest as if she was scared it would be ripped from her arms.

And where was the mother?

Alexander scowled as his mind worked. It wasn't his business he knew, but could he help it if the woman inexplicably fascinated him? It was obvious that she'd been independent from a very young age...but why? Where was her father now? And had her mother ever been present?

To he, whose mother's death drove him towards his current goals, family was everything. His father was an overbearing, meddlesome man but Alexander wouldn't trade him for the world. And anyone who knew anything about him knew how much he had adored his mother.

But what did family mean to Cece?

"Is there any more pizza left, Alexander? Xaviar's stomach is like a bottomless -" He turned, watching Cece slow at the foot of the stairs as she took him in. When her dark eyes fell on the picture in his hand, she seemed to stiffen, her entire body seizing with tension. As sensitive as Alexander knew she was about her monetary and familial situation, he'd never seen her tensed up the way she was now. At the sight of her stiff body, he had to resist the urge to soothe away the stress with his hands and mouth.

This was hardly the place, or the time.

Slowly, he set down the photo where he'd found it, his eyes never leaving her. "My apologies. I didn't mean to pry."

She seemed to be fighting some sort of inner battle with herself beneath his gaze. Cecilia took a deep breath, gazing from him to the controversial picture and then back again. Slowly, painstakingly, she crossed the room to stand by his side, her eyes locked on the image. "You're..." She swallowed thickly, visibly trying to get a handle on her emotions. "You're not prying. It's just a picture." She picked up the plain wooden frame, her eyes roving over each and every face within it. "A picture of my dad and I...and Xaviar. He's only about two months here."

Alexander nodded. He knew he was now treading on thin ice...but so long as Cecilia was talking, he wanted to keep it that way.

"I assume...you've raised Xaviar for most of his life?"

A short, harsh laugh escaped the young woman. "Most of his life? I've raised him his *entire* life. I changed his diapers and cleaned up his messes. I pureed his food and worked two jobs to make sure he could make all of his doctor's visits. I..." She trailed off, shaking her head as she closed her eyes tightly.

Alexander gave her a moment, his own chest tightening at the visceral pain on her lovely face. "My father was never here. And I suppose...you might as well now...its because he's in jail. And he'll be there for a long, long time."

He knew better than to ask why.

The man in the picture Cecilia held had the sunken look of a drug addict – a man who would abandon his own family for the next high. In his line of work, Alexander had seen dozens of his kind.

Cristina Grenier

They were another component to the city's dark underbelly, and watching them rip lives apart...rip *his* life apart...

It was enough to infuriate him.

But Cecilia didn't need his anger now. She needed his understanding. The imploring look in her eyes spoke volumes of exactly how she expected him to respond to her admission. He was a man who put drug pushers away – who reveled in cleaning up streets and taking out the trash.

Her father had been a part of that trash – and it was evident in the way she reacted to even a mere picture of the man that she despised him for it.

The picture he'd been forming in his mind of his hard-working PA had just become leagues clearer than it had been before. She had taken her brother in at a tender age to care for him, rather than see him stolen away by the system that was supposed to keep him safe. She'd had everything under control when the economy had dealt her a blow that had shattered both her pride and finances.

And he had helped her begin to dig her way out. Now, the reason she had looked at him with such relief and gratitude the day he'd hired her was evident.

She was proud, independent, and she was hurting.

Almost as badly, he would venture to say, as he hurt over the premature death of his mother.

How could he judge her for something that had nothing to do with her life and the way she lived it? And how many people before him had judged her for the father who had probably torn her childhood apart?

Righting Wrongs

Without a word, Alexander reached down to pull Cecilia's form against him. She was warm and pliant in his arms, and the moment he enveloped her in his embrace, her body began to soften. The tension slowly eased away as she buried her face in his chest.

For what seemed like an eternity, neither of them spoke.

When Cecilia did open her mouth, however, her voice was soft, almost inaudible. "Thank you."

Alexander's lips quirked slightly as he looked down on her, before tipped her chin up to meet her gaze.

"For working you like the devil?"

A soft laugh escaped her at his jest. "For working me at all." The genuine gratitude in his voice moved him in a way he hadn't been in what seemed like an eternity. For Alexander, his work had been his life for as long as he could remember. Though Cecilia had begun as a distraction, now, she was becoming something dangerously different.

An need.

"You're welcome." The urge to kiss her was almost overpowering, but Alexander did not want an irked fourteen-year old trying to put him into an early grave. She had come home early to spend time with her brother, and he would not monopolize that time.

But later, when the pizza was gone and the time for restraint had passed...she was all his.

Cristina Grenier

CHAPTER 7 - REALITY

He needed her.

Badly.

It seemed like ages since he'd had her in his bed though Alexander knew it couldn't have been more than a week. They were working on a particularly difficult case and, as such, they hadn't had much time to be together privately. Additionally, Cecilia found herself wrapped up in planning for her brother's school trip, for which she had to allot funds and arrange transportation.

Though he knew how important the boy was to her, he couldn't help but be slightly jealous.

"Are you there, Xander?"

His father's voice on the line jerked him back to the present. The man had called him in the middle of the day, asking about his Easter plans. The question was posed every year, and had grown somewhat redundant, as Alexander never had any plans. Growing up, he had always anticipated Easter with his mother – her cooking, enthusiasm and love always served to bring the family closer. Since she'd passed, his father had attempted to replicate the experience, but it had never been the same.

Still, he made the trip out to the manor every spring, as he did every Christmas, in order to be with the older man when he knew he would miss his wife most prevalently.

His father needed him – and it was a call he would always answer.

Righting Wrongs

"I'm here, Dad."

"Yeah, like I was saying...there's this girl Charlotte who I really want you to meet." Alexander repressed a groan. Would his father never stop trying to set him up with women who he believed were shining examples of the female sex?

It seemed as if the man dug up a new woman every month, and every month, Alexander came up with excuses.

He hadn't actually gone on a date with a woman since Cecilia had begun to work for him. While before, dating had seemed mundane and tedious to him, he knew that now, it would be impossible. How could he force himself to waste his time on another woman when the one that most fascinated him worked at his side all day? How could he fathom sating his lusts with someone he'd just met when Cecilia continued to surprise him with each day that passed?

He'd staved off his father as diplomatically as he could...but the fact of the matter was, the man would never give up until Alexander admitted that there was a woman he was interested in. At the prospect, the district attorney clenched the edge of his desk.

The *only* woman who'd held his interest in the past decade was seated not ten feet from him.

How was he supposed to explain to his father that he was too absorbed in his PA to flatter socialites and pander to their vain, ceaseless prattle?

All at once, he froze on the spot.

Wait just one moment.

That was...exactly what he would do.

Why the hell shouldn't he tell his old man about Cecilia? It wasn't as if she was some air-headed hotel heiress after the power or status that his name conferred. The woman was embarrassed to be seen with him and public and warned him that if she ever ended up on a tabloid, she'd have his head. She cared about her job, she cared about her brother...and he'd like to believe that she cared just a little bit about pleasing him.

Proving to his father that he wasn't the asexual workaholic that the elder man thought him to be? That would please him immensely.

"Actually, Dad, I've met someone."

The words felt just as strange leaving his mouth as he'd thought they would; and from the shocked silence on the other side of the line, they seemed to be words his father hadn't ever thought to hear him say.

It was definitely interesting, for once, to have shocked his old man into speechlessness.

Alexander smiled, waiting for his father to speak. He had almost forgotten what it was like to genuinely surprise someone.

"You...you've met a woman?"

"I have." He stared out of the window of his anteroom upon the slender line of Cecilia's spine as she bent over her laptop. Today she wore a mustard yellow dress that complimented the hue of her skin and brought color to the entire office. "She's actually the PA I've been speaking to you about."

"Your PA?" If anything, the man sounded even more surprised. He, of all people, knew how sacred the workplace was to his son. For Alexander to have overlooked that sanctity in order to be with someone he'd hired himself, well...the District Attorney was sure that his father could do the math. "So this entire time, you've been seeing Melody's replacement?"

The skepticism in his father's voice was extremely pronounced, making Alexander wince. He realized that he hadn't ever given his father very many details about Cecilia's appearance. Only her work ethic and her dedication. His old man very probably thought he'd suddenly developed an interest in mature women.

He shuddered at the thought. Melody had been well on her way to sixty – a bit older than his tastes ran.

"Dad, she's substantially younger than Melody....and yes, I've been...seeing her for quite a while."

Was that what he was doing, truly? "Seeing" Cecilia? He wouldn't insult her so much as to say she was just a passing fling. No, in the past few months, the woman had captured and held his attention far more acutely than any before her. However, he knew that what was between them was still beyond definition. They were lovers, certainly...but beyond that...he had no idea.

"Well, then. You should bring her to the house for Easter dinner."

Shit.

Though he'd known the request was coming, actually hearing it made him cringe slightly. He'd *never* brought a woman home, and while it was only natural that his father ask him to prove that he did, in fact, *have* romantic interests, allowing Cecilia to meet the man – to see the wreckage that remained of his family life...it gave him slight pause.

It was, he realized after a moment, slightly hypocritical of him. No doubt she'd felt the same way about allowing him into her home – and Cecilia, as with everything she did, had handled the challenge admirably.

There was no reason he couldn't do the same.

"This Sunday, right?" The words came out even calmer than he'd hoped, bolstering his courage.

"Yep. Bring the potato salad."

It was the one thing that their housekeeper, Marisol, had difficulties making. He nodded. "Of course."

He reassured his father that he wouldn't beg off at the last moment or come up with any excuses before hanging up the phone. Once he'd done so, Alexander exhaled hotly, running a hand through his dark blonde hair. Well, he'd done it. He'd made the first step towards introducing a woman to his father. Now, all he had to do was to get Cecilia to agree to come with him.

He was sure it would be easier said than done.

"This is *amazing*."

Bent over the amazingly decadent chocolate gateau he had ordered as the last course to their meal, Alexander glanced over at the woman across from him, who was busy divesting her plate of every last scrap of the dessert. For a moment, the district attorney watched, transfixed, as Cecilia's tongue wrapped around her fork to lick it clean.

Righting Wrongs

He'd invited her over for dinner tonight not only to have her close at hand for his own physical needs, but in order to broach the subject of Easter dinner with her – and he knew that he was liable to forget all about that particular line of questioning if the woman didn't stop making love to her gateau.

It still stunned him, how he'd taken her to bed so many times and still, his hunger for her only seemed to grow stronger with each passing day. He found himself thinking of her far more, now, than he mulled over the numerous cases that he managed every day – of her, her brother, and the way she worked whole-heartedly towards her goals without expecting anyone to do anything for her. He'd grown to crave the sight of her toffee-hued skin sliding against his every moment he wasn't with her.

This, he knew, was more than a little dangerous.

His reputation as an unfeeling, workaholic hard ass was faltering – and it was all her fault.

"Please tell me there's more." At her plea, his lips quirked in amusement. He'd learned a while ago about the woman's weakness for chocolate, and since discovering it, he'd probably exploited it more than his fair share.

Tonight, however, he wasn't admitting to the extra gateau in the fridge.

Not yet.

Without a word, he stood to round the table to her side. When Cecilia looked up at him, the hunger that colored her gaze had him repressing a groan. Had she really ever believed that he couldn't be attracted to her? Those large, honey eyes, full lips, and curvacious form? The woman might be secretive about her life but she kept no secrets from him in the bedroom.

He wouldn't allow it.

Taking her hand, he guided her to her feet a moment before his mouth found hers. She tasted of chocolate, sweet and savory, spiced with the wine they'd had along with their dinner. He'd taken it upon himself to see that she ate properly, knowing that she often gave her younger brother her share of food to keep his strength up; if anything, since he'd taken her diet into his own hands, her curves had grown even more lush.

Her hips flared alluringly below a tiny waist and her breasts plumped against his hands. Groaning, Alexander deepened the kiss, sweeping the plates they'd used aside to set her atop the table, drawing her even more closely against him.

His hands pushed the heavy wool of her skirt up and over her thighs, baring the soft, pliant skin to his hands. The moment he touched her, Cecilia shuddered, moaning as he sucked her lower lip between his teeth to tease for a moment. Her hands raised to tunnel through his hair, mussing it from the strict, slicked back style he'd worn the entire day.

She liked to unravel him, he'd found – to muss his shirt, undo his buttons and tear off his clothes until he was hardly recognizable as the public figure he played every day. Now, she undid his tie, tossing it aside before pushing his jacket down his arms until it pooled on the polished marble floor. Before she could go any further, however, he stopped her long enough to strip her dress over her head, leaving her in a set of wispy white lingerie that he'd had to demand she take from him when he'd gifted it to her.

Righting Wrongs

Seeing her in the lacy underwear was more than worth the argument they'd had. The balconet cups of the bra pressed her breasts upward and together for his feasting, while the matching Brazilian bottoms exposed more than they covered. He'd made sure to remove the price tag on the expensive lingerie, lest she have even more reason to fight him over it.

As far as he was concerned, it didn't matter if he'd paid twenty dollars or two hundred for the luxurious garb. Seeing her so scantily clad – and knowing it was for him? It was all worth it.

Tearing his mouth from hers, Alexander kissed down the length of her neck to the deep vee of her cleavage. There, he inhaled the tantalizing scent of her a moment before peeling the near insubstantial cups of the bra from her breasts to expose their dark, perfectly round peaks.

When he sucked one of them into the heat of his mouth, Cecilia squirmed, gasping as her fingers curled into his shoulders. She tasted utterly divine – musky and sweet – he could drug himself on her very presence.

She arched into his administrations as he drew upon the peak of one breast and then the other before lifting her into his arms to carry down the hall towards the bedroom.

The first time he'd ever brought her here, Cecilia had looked around his apartment in awe. She'd been astounded by the high ceilings and endless space, where he simply found it reminded him of the isolated life he'd chosen to live. Now, she was much more comfortable, and her presence, he found, served to have the same affect on he himself.

The dark-skinned woman yanked on his clothes as he deposited her on the bed, ripping his shirt from his slacks before popping the buttons so they zinged off randomly in the room. Growling at her eagerness, he crawled onto the bed to pin her beneath his larger form, his eyes locked on her parted lips and wide eyes.

She knew he was stronger than her - that he could pinion her body against the bed and take her until she screamed for succor. But, that wasn't what he wanted tonight.

No, tonight, he would take her slowly – savor her. How was he to know what the next day might bring – or even the next hour? The woman could very well refuse his request and flee his apartment, and he wouldn't blame her. Things between them had become far too intimate and too involved for him to pretend that he could cut them off at any time he liked.

Beneath the scant underwear, she was wet and wanting for him. When his fingers slid over her entrance, her breath hitched and she threw her head back, her magnificent dark curls spilling over his pillow.

He loved this...craved her soft gasps and whimpers as he slid inside her – the way she opened up completely to him in the throes or orgasm...

When his mouth found the heated, damp folds between her legs, she cried out, her fingers grasping his hair for dear life as he tasted her. Her desire was intoxicating against his tongue – almost as sweet as the chocolate they'd consumed just moments ago. When she squirmed, seeking escape, he pinned her hips to the bed, drawing a helpless whimper from her. Cecilia knew, by this point, that he would eat her until he was finished, whether that time last five minutes or five hours.

By the time he'd had his fill, his lips were slick with her arousal, her body trembling from the skill of his mouth. She clung to him as he slid inside her, her eyes sliding closed as her inner muscles squeezed him exquisitely.

This was what he lived for.

"Look at me." He ordered lowly, watching as she fought the haze of pleasure that drifted over her to focus intently on his green gaze. "Watch me, Cecilia."

She inhaled sharply as he pressed deep, his hips sliding against hers. One hand tangled in her copious curls as he drew her gaze back to his. Her curves slid against the hard lines of his body, pale skin against deep, smooth caramel. He felt her clenching tighter and tighter around him, stealing his sanity to send sparks along the surface of his skin.

When she came, the delicious grip of her around his engorged flesh was enough to trigger his own release, and, with a sharp, low sound of pleasure, Alexander jerked his hips against hers as he emptied himself within her willing body.

It was only after, much after, that he revealed to her the existence of the additional gateau.

She glared at him, slapping his arm as he mentioned it before dragging him to the kitchen for a second helping of the dessert. He supposed, however, that he couldn't complain. As Cecilia indulged in the chocolate confection, she stood before him completely naked.

He took in the curves of her form hungrily, trying to remember that he'd had an aim for the evening. It wasn't until she had popped the last of the gateau into her succulent mouth that he finally cleared his mind enough to recall his father's request.

Cristina Grenier

"Cecilia?"

"Mmm?"

Setting her gleaming, clean spoon down on the counter, she turned to face him, and he struggled to keep from rising in his sweatpants at the sight of her nude, glorious form.

Once upon a time, Alexander had thought himself beyond nervousness. He had faced opponents in courtrooms who had threatened his life and screamed insults at him. He had faced doubt and indecision and been questioned by men in high places. But he had never felt his stomach twisting the way it did now in apprehension.

"My family...my father and I...we traditionally have Easter dinner together at the family home in the country. I thought you might like to join us this year."

For a moment, she just stared at him, her bright eyes inscrutable. For the thirty seconds in which she didn't speak, Alexander was utterly certain she'd refuse. Then, slowly, the dark-skinned woman arched a brow.

"Are you asking me to come as your PA?"

The question was a diplomatic one, and he admired her for it. He knew he'd have to answer her truthfully.

"I'm asking to introduce you to my father. As my PA...and as the woman I"m currently involved with." Cecilia gave him a slow once over, from head to toe, as if trying to find the lie in his statement. When she could see nothing but the truth laid bare in his gaze, a slow smile curved her full mouth. Leisurely, she sauntered over him, using the full brunt of her allure, before she wrapped her arms around his neck.

Righting Wrongs

"I suppose I have to say yes. I'm supposed to go wherever you do, after all."

For the first time since his youth, Alexander resisted the urge to bray in triumph. Instead, he merely lifted his lover into her arms and against him, pressing his mouth to hers as he kissed her deeply. Success soon turned into rekindled desire, and as he lead her back towards the bedroom, he couldn't recall feeling so light.

Not since before his mother had been taken from him.

**

Xaviar was utterly elated.

In the past two months he'd made over two thousand dollars doing running for Malcolm. The boy was far more connected than he'd ever have imagined, and despite his reservations at first, it was relatively easy to slip through their south Brooklyn neighborhood unseen.

As he gazed at the bills stacked up on his desk, he smiled.

At least three quarters of the money would go to Cece.

She'd been working her butt off for the past half a year working for her stick-up-the-ass boss. The man who, it was quite clear, had a thing for his sister.

He frowned at the thought.

Sure, the guy bought home decent pizza every once in a while, but did he think he could win Xaviar over with food alone?

Cristina Grenier

Her certainly hoped not. If he was interested in Cece, he would have to provide. Stop working her like a dog and start treating her like the amazing woman she really was.

Even at his tender age, Xaviar could tell the difference between a girl who wanted to go places in her life, and one without ambition. This was all because of his sister. The woman had never set her bar any lower than the highest she could possibly achieve, and she'd taught him to do the same.

With this money, hopefully they could jump start their journey out of the ghetto and back up to Harlem. God knew, whatever tight-ass Cross paid her wasn't enough. She was *just* getting to the point where her bills were back on track.

He knew because, like all curious teenagers, he'd peeked at their mail.

His sister had college debts, rent, water and gas to catch up on, and he was going to do the best he possibly could to help her.

He'd keep only a small amount of money for himself – for drawing supplies and the video game subscription he hoped to purchase. On the server, he hoped to meet up with a few of his old friends from his gifted school and find out how things were there. *Maybe* he could even start telling them to prepare for his return. According to Cece, change for them was only drawing closer.

He was so taken with his triumph that he almost didn't notice the when his phone buzzed on his desk. Carefully, he placed all of the money in his top drawer before flipping open the screen.

It was a message from Malcolm.

Hey man. Wassup? Got a real big job coming up. Next Monday, during lunch break. U in?

Xaviar immediately frowned. If Malcolm wanted him to run during lunch break, that meant that he would be on school time – time he'd rather not take.

But...a big job meant higher pay. More money that he could give to his sister, and less time spent in their drafty, roach infested apartment.

It was just one day, right? One time, and then he'd be back to odd side runs after school. He'd be careful, as he always was.

His lips quirking into a tentative smile, the teen returned the text.

I'm in.

"Xaviar?" He jumped at his sister's voice from downstairs. For the past thirty minutes, the succulent smell of fried chicken had been wafting up the stairs. "Dinner time!"

With the promise of a full belly and stuffed coffers, the teen grinned, replacing his phone on the desk to rush downstairs to his meal.

**

"I'm nervous."

"Don't be."

"You have *got* to be kidding me. Your driveway's longer than my entire street."

Alexander couldn't help but smirk at Cecilia's exaggeration. Yes, the drive up to the manor was long, but considering the house was only one in a large community of homes, it was impossible for it to be longer than a road in Brooklyn.

It was a gorgeous spring day – the sun was shining and the trees were just beginning to flower along the side of the road. When they finally crested the drive to pull to a stop before the manor, he was consumed with nostalgia.

He had grown up here.

The large brick house with its green shutters and carefully manicured lawn was just as much a part of him as the courtroom. He remembered breaking windows and once spilling a bag of fertilizer into the fountain that decorated the area by the garage. His mother had sentenced him to a week in his room.

He'd snuck out anyway.

The thought drew a a brief smile.

There were enough memories here to keep her alive...when he chose to focus on them. For his father, he was sure it was easier to focus on how she'd died in this very house, her blood splattering the walls and their minds forever.

"Hey."

He turned, jarred from his macabre thoughts to see Cecilia looking up at him, her expression concerned. "Are you alright?"

A large container of her own homemade potato salad rested on her lap, and the sight of it served to help his good humor return. He'd been intent on purchasing some store brand, but she had convinced him that hers was a staple at every block party she'd brought it too.

He'd tasted the rich dish while she wasn't looking, and Alexander would have to say that it was pretty ridiculously amazing. "Are you ready?" He arched a brow at her, hoping to change the subject.

"As I'm going to be." With a small smile, the dark-skinned woman slid from the car, trying not to gape at her surroundings. While Alexander couldn't profess that his family home was the most luxurious in the community, he knew it was no use trying to profess that his family wasn't wealthy. His mother had been of the French upper class and his father a ranking officer in the military for a number of years.

He'd been well-rounded, with both of them to influence him.

Taking Cecilia's arm, he led her to the front door, where he rang the bell.

It was only a few moments before his father answered.

Edward Cross was taller, even, than his son. Due to vigorous workouts, he remained unbowed by age, even well into his sixties. His green eyes were sharp and his blonde hair graying, but he still remained quite the presence. "Alex!" The man reached forward to envelop his son in a massive hug and Alexander let him, relishing in the warmth. He rarely ever had such close contact with people, and though his father could get on his nerves, he still loved the man devotedly. "You made it! And you'e brought your...friend."

The man's booming voice faltered on the word and Alexander was immediately on his guard as he watched his father take in Cecilia at his side. She'd worn a dark brown dress that reached her knees with a modest collar – the outfit was just form-fitting enough to reveal her attractive figure while complimenting her skin and bright eyes. He, for one, though that she looked gorgeous.

He could see that his father was thinking something else entirely.

Alexander had to admit that he'd never paused to consider exactly what his father would think of his involvement with a black woman. The man tended to stick to his golf buddies and their circles, which were pretty monochromatic. The only person of color he'd ever had any interaction with was, sadly, the man who had killed his wife. Edward Cross had never been to a slum, never seen the way that blacks could be marginalized and put down simply for the stereotypes they'd been branded with.

If anything, he'd been the ultimate victim of such stereotypes.

Alexander realized that, perhaps, this dinner wasn't going to go as well as he had planned.

"I'm Cecilia Thompson, Mr. Cross." Cecilia herself seemed to be taking the meeting carefully. She shifted her potato salad to one hand to extend the other for his father to shake. Edward looked her over slowly, from head to toe, before tentatively gripping her hand for perhaps half a second. The contact left both Cecilia and Alexander tense as his father turned away.

"You can just put your salad on the table, there." He gestured to a table in the entryway – no where near the kitchen. The movement very clearly pronounced that he had no intention to even try it.

Righting Wrongs

Alexander frowned as Cecilia did as he asked before stepping after him into the house.

He hadn't even invited her in.

Cecilia caught Alexander's eye nervously as she stepped over the threshold, and he attempted a reassuring smile. The front entryway of the house smelled, as it always did, like lavender and roses. His mother had adored fresh flowers, and so his father maintained them.

Hanging behind the staircase that led the the upper floors was an immense family portrait – one of Alexander's favorite images of his family. In it, he was seated between his parents at age sixteen, his blonde hair a mess, his soccer ball clutched tightly in his arms. His mother, a classical French beauty, leaned over him, her long mahogany tresses spilling down her back, blue eyes bright with mirth. His father looked happier than Alexander had seen him since that day, smiling and proud of his family, not hint of gray in his hair, resplendent in his military garb.

"Is that...is that her?"

Gazing up at the picture in awe, Cecilia stepped forward to take it in. Alexander's stomach twisted as he realized it was the first time she had seen an image of his mother. Everyone in the office, including Cecilia, knew that the woman's death had driven him to be what he was.

Cecilia was perhaps the only person, however, to know how deeply the event still affected him. He spoke little of it, but there were nights where he woke stiff, hardly breathing, only to have her hold him in her arms until he calmed.

"She's beautiful." Cecilia took in the slender, ageless woman in her dark blue shift, and Alexander knew that she hadn't commented on his mother to flatter her or express her pity; she was truly moved by the deceased woman's youth and radiance.

Amelie Cross had that effect on everyone – up until the day she died.

"She *was* beautiful." As Edward cross came up next to Cecilia, her attention was drawn to him. Though Alexander had spent previous little time with his father since he'd become district attorney, he liked to believe that he still knew the man – that he was still the same loving individual who had raised him.

However, the deep sneer that now colored the elder man's face was an expression he'd never seen before. It was anger, grief, and frustration all bottled into one body – and he knew it could hardly bode well for their guest. "She was *gorgeous*, until one of *your* people killed her. Has Alex ever told you how it happened? How some *thug* broke into this house and shot my wife for the diamond necklace she was wearing? The gift I gave her for our twentieth wedding anniversary? Has he told you how she bled, fear in her eyes, while the man escaped, before dying in my goddamn arms?"

"Dad." Alexander's word thrummed with dangerous warning.

His heart beat wildly in his chest as he watched, shocked at his father's violent reaction to Cecilia's mere presence. "Don't *Dad* me." Edward's reply came just as sharply as he swung around on his son. "I've been trying to set you up with a good girl for years and *this* is what you bring home? This ghetto hussy? How could you defile this house, Alexander? Your mother *died* here, gunned own

Righting Wrongs

by *her* type." The finger he thrust in Cecilia's direction trembled with rage.

For her part, the wide-eyed woman only stared at his father in shock, hurt evident in her features. Cecilia wasn't one prone to crying, or outlandish displays of emotion, but she didn't have to be for Alexander to know how deeply his father's words had injured her.

"Dad, you don't even *know* her." His voice was low, his own ire raising now. "She does an amazing job in my office and helps convict men like the ones who killed mom – ensuring that they don't hurt anyone ever again."

"She helps you while she warns others away. Can't you see, son, she's just in your office to gather information to take back to all her little black friends. How to stay away, how to avoid getting caught – she's using you. You'll see it soon enough."

"Mr. Cross."

Cecilia's voice rang through the foyer, loud and firm.

Even as Alexander registered she was speaking, he was trying to reconcile that the man before him and the father he loved were the same person. Certainly, Edward had uttered some extreme things in his lifetime, but this?

He'd never imagined that his mother's death had so detrimentally jaded the man.

Now, both he and his father stared at Cecilia, who looked from one of them to the other, her expression unreadable. "I'm sorry about what happened to your wife, Mr. Cross. I truly am. But you have to understand, that does not give you the right to project your fears onto every person of color that you meet. I've never touched drugs in my life and I've never committed a criminal offense. I can think of no nobler cause than helping your son put away criminals like the one that took your wife from you. I don't know what else I can tell you to make you see people of color differently, but it's evident enough that I'm not welcome here. I'll see myself out."

Alexander watched the woman take a deep, steadying breath, before she turned on her heel to exit the way she came, her head held high.

The moment the door closed behind her, Edward's gaze fell to his son. His green eyes were livid, blind with rage and hatred "Don't you see, son? She comes into our house and disrespects me. The *last* thing you need is a woman like that."

Alexander closed his eyes for a moment, trying to gather his emotions. He had always been able to control himself, both in the courtroom and out. There had been times where he'd wanted to strangle full grown men, hunt down pimps and murder them in cold blood...but he had never lost the facade of strength that enveloped him.

Not until now.

"The last thing I need is a father like *you*, Dad." Shock colored Edward's face the moment the word's left Alexander's mouth. "You think you're *honoring* Mom's memory by spouting this racist bullshit hate? One man, *one man,* gunned her down. He could have been white, he could have been latino, he could have been fucking Amish, but he happened to be black. That is *no* excuse for you to treat people of color like this – and especially not Cecilia. She is the *only* one that has helped me come to terms with your wife's death, as you seem to absorbed in sequestering yourself in the manor and trying to keep her alive than actually helping me reach my goals.

"I can't beat the truth out of people, Dad, and maintaining this narrow belief you've somehow acquired that all people of color are out to do you harm isn't helping you, and it isn't helping me. I don't want some trumped up Manhattan socialite full of herself, after whatever she thinks I can provide her with until she tires of me. I want Cecilia, and until you're ready to talk about her like a human instead of a goddamn hate Parrot, we're through."

The look on his father's face, from the raw pain in his eyes to his wide open mouth, made Alexander want to take back his words and the force behind them, but he knew that would help neither his father nor himself. Instead, he merely turned his back on the man who had raised him and stormed from the house, both his color and heart rate high.

The moment he was out in the warm sun, he rushed for the car. He didn't know where Cecilia had gotten to, but it couldn't be far. He could catch up with her and he would apologize -

Alexander froze when he took in her tall figure seated in the passenger seat of his Mercedes, staring straight ahead at his family home. Without a word, he opened the door to slide into the driver's seat.

For a moment, neither of them said anything.

He took in the tight muscles of Cecilia's body, from her firmly set mouth to her hands clasped tightly on her lap. Her entire form was utterly rigid – at least as much so as his own.

He had to force himself to relax.

Reaching over, he placed a hand gently over hers, looking down at her as he contemplated what he could possibly say to make this right. He was torn – part of him wanted nothing more than to go back inside and shake some sense into his father, while the other knew that leaving Cecilia at this moment would be the worst mistake he could ever make.

"Cecilia..."

"Don't call me that!" Her voice was surprisingly sharp as she jerked away from him, her breath hitching. "My name is Cece. Just Cece."

It was what everyone else in the office called her – something he'd never picked up. To him, she appeared regal and capable – much more a Cecilia than any nickname she could shorten her title to.

In this instant, he realized that the moniker defined her more than he had ever considered. To her brother, who no doubt adored her, she was Cece. To Margaret, who looked up to her, she was Cece. He had put her on a pedestal refusing to believe that she could be hurt or shaken, when at the end of the day, all she wanted was to be the woman who provided and cared for those important to her.

"Cece..." The name felt strange on his tongue, but somehow comforting. "I'm sorry. Please believe me when I tell you I had no idea my father would behave the way he did."

She only nodded stiffly, refusing to look at him.

"You know me. He didn't raise me with that kind of hatred and I've never abided by it. It's just...he hasn't been the same since my mother's death. I should have spent more time with him. I...I could have prevented this."

He let the guilt consume him.

It was easier to feel guilt over his own shortcomings that to contemplate what his father had become in his absence. He'd been so wrapped up in waging his war against Manhattan's seedy underbelly that he'd neglected to care for one of it's most wronged victims.

"Don't blame yourself." When Cecilia did speak, her tone was soft, almost inaudible. Slowly, she turned her hands to take his between hers. "I...I know he was hurt. And I know that the man who killed your mother wasn't served proper justice."

"The doesn't excuse what he said." Alexander returned almost immediately, his tone vehement. "And it never will. *You* didn't kill my mother. It's very evident that my father...his solitude has gotten to him. He needs help...and I need to provide it."

For a moment, silence reigned in the car.

When Cece's head finally came down on his shoulder, the tension easing from his body, a low sigh escaped him.

How could he have been so blind?

He should have forseen this issue, and now, because he hadn't, he was going to have to make it up to her...and deal with his father's aberrant and incorrect state of mind. Had he really been so absorbed in his work that he hadn't seen this? Certainly, the man always encouraged dangerous acts of vandalism and violence, but to know that it was not only against those who deserved to be prosecuted, but against all people of color?

He would have to find a good psychiatrist, and fast.

Seeing his father railing at an innocent woman, his anger fueled by grief and loss, had disturbed him. It wasn't something he wanted to risk again. "Cece, I have learned in my line of work that you can never judge anyone by the color of their skin. You can't judge them by their parentage, their ethnicity, or where they come from. My father is wrong, and I promise I will set him right."

She nodded against his shoulder before looking up at him.

He watched the pain and desolation slowly melt from her honey eyes, and resolved to waste not one moment putting his father back on the right path. He would take time off from work, if need be, and he would with the man for as long as required.

It was important to him – and to any future he might have with Cece.

"Can we...go back to my place?" Cece's inquiry surprised him and he arched a brow. Agter this fiasco, he would think she'd wanted nothing more than to return home alone. "I just...I don't want Easter to end like this. I can cook, we can have dinner with Xaviar, and later...later we can work on this."

Leaning down, Alexander pressed his lips to hers softly, impressed, as always, by the resolve of his PA.

"Of course. I'll get the groceries." For a moment, she scowled at him, before the expression slowly gave way to a small smile.

"Fine. But I'm not getting anything organic or fancy."

So she professed.

Righting Wrongs

As they started back down his drive, headed toward Manhattan, Alexander resolved to buy her the best ingredients he could find – arguing with her over groceries would keep his mind from his father, and from the pain he had caused a woman Alexander had come to care for deeply.

Cristina Grenier

CHAPTER 8 - FRACTURE

"He's *what?*"

Cecilia repressed a smile as Margaret stared down at her, the thin girl's eyes wide. She was currently in the middle of gathering dirt on Alexander's newest defendant. The man was convinced that Alexander couldn't turn him into a stool pigeon with a terrifying sentence. With her intel, not only was the D.A poised to do just that, Macmillan would be spilling information out of every orifice in his body once he saw the alternative.

However, despite her ground-breaking work on this case, Alexander himself was not present.

He'd taken the day off.

In the months that she'd been working with the man, even the mention of a personal day had earned her a death glare. However, this particular day was one that the man was spending with his father.

"He's off, Margaret. Just for today. Family issues."

That was the understatement of the century.

Remembering how the gigantic Edward Cross had reacted to her presence in his house was enough to make her stomach clench in discomfort.

Living in New York, there were precious few times in her life that Cece had been confronted about her race. She'd tried to provide an open and caring environment for her brother and had never judged anyone for the mere color of their skin.

Righting Wrongs

She could understand Mr. Cross' devastation. His wife had died in his arms, victim of a horrible crime. However, she could not condone the way he had acted towards her. Though her words to the man had been brave, she didn't think she'd ever felt so small as when he'd demeaned her in front of Alexander.

Worst of all was that she'd had to face the prospect that the man couldn't very well disown his own father. As she'd sat in the car, waiting for Alexander, her mind had tortured her with what he might be saying to placate the man – how he might condone the man's behavior, making excuses for him.

Alexander had done no such thing.

Instead, he had apologized, immediately recognizing his father's need for rehabilitation. At the thought, Cece frowned. The guilt on the man's face had pained her own heart. It was quite obvious that Alexander blamed his work-obsessed nature for the hatred his father had developed. Before she had arrived, she knew, the man had hardly ever left his office unless it was for a necessary social function or to visit the court house.

She could imagine what she might feel like if something similar happened with Xaviar. She'd question herself, her parenting skills, and she wouldn't rest until she had addressed the problem. In Alexander's position, helping to rehabilitate his father required time away from the courtroom and the vendetta that had driven his career.

She knew how much of a sacrifice it was for him, and it was clear that his father's adopted attitude disturbed him. Though she was sure he'd enjoyed the Easter dinner she'd made for he and Xaviar, the man had brooded through the entire meal.

Xaviar, for his part, had been amazingly upbeat. He'd eaten his way through several large helpings of roast lamb with barely a suspicious glance at Alexander. Cece was left to wonder how much longer she planned to wait before revealing the true nature of their relationship to the boy. While not completely warm toward her boss, her brother seemed to tolerate him well enough. She could only hope that the boy could at least be happy for her. If he wasn't the biggest fan of the man himself, she could tempt him with a fact she herself was just coming to accept:

She was happier than she'd been since she'd lost her job.

Even through her experience with Alexander's father, and the trials he pushed her through in the office, it was hard for Cece to deny the way the man made her feel. Certainly, his immense, commanding presence still made her warm between the legs – even months after their first interlude – but there was something more.

He made her laugh – perhaps more than he actually meant to, but the man's stubbornness was in and of itself something humorous. His drive and perseverance to clean up streets that threatened she and her brother every day was something she could appreciate on a very personal level; and though the D.A put up a front that no one would ever question, she knew that his mother's death still haunted him, proving that buried beneath layers of emotional distance, the man was still very human.

It was his humanity that endeared him to her. Beyond his stunning good looks, his success, and his drive, the Alexander she admired most was the one that held her close, late at night, and told her that he feared he would fail.

She loved him.

It was something that she could hardly admit to herself, but with every passing day, the truth solidified more in her mind.

Here was a man who had intimidated her – who had pushed her beyond her limits. Who had asked everything of her and still desired more...and she couldn't see her life without him. When she rose in the morning, she was excited to come into the office. Law wasn't her field, and never would be, but she'd found a new cause in helping Alexander reach his goals.

His convictions had become hers.

Just as somehow, inexplicably, he'd stolen her heart.

Even now, she missed him. Without his presence, the office felt somehow empty. She knew Margaret might be breathing a sigh of relief, but she herself felt somehow bereft.

Tomorrow would come soon enough, she wagered. The moment he came in, she would present him with the information she'd come across. His smile would brighten her day and she could look forward to dinner with him.

Dinner and dessert.

The thought made her lips curve slightly and above her, Margaret laughed softly. "What, are you going to invite your boyfriend into the office now that Big Bad Cross is away?"

Cece hoped that the flush on her face didn't give her away. So far, she and Alexander had done well to keep their interludes out of the office. If Margaret knew just how intimate she was with the man the girl so feared, Cece was sure she would flip.

Better to keep it secret.

Cristina Grenier

Especially since she was just coming to terms with her feelings for the man herself.

The day passed uneventfully. With Alexander absent from the office, the overall vibe was much more relaxed, but Cece found herself itching to go home. She wanted nothing more than to find something with the D.A's scent on it and curl up in front of the spotty TV.

She drove home humming to herself and picked up Chinese takeout on the way. Her funds were just now at the point where she could begin to think about saving anew – to contemplate leaving her seedy south Brooklyn neighborhood and getting Xaviar back on track in a better school.

When she returned home, however, her brother was absent.

It wasn't terribly unusual. These days, Xaviar often stayed after school to sell his candy. Cece grinned when she remembered the crushed tens he presented he with every week. The boy's birthday was in a month, and she intended to return every cent of his money inside a clever card. She'd probably start looking for a good one in the next week or two.

Cece had just settled on the couch, wrapped in an immense jacket that Alexander had lent her, when the doorbell rang. The dark-skinned woman frowned, turning her head from the news to rise. She wasn't expecting anyone, and if it was some crackhead trying to clean her windows or looking for a dollar, she meant to turn them away.

However, when she opened her door, she found the man she'd missed all day on her doorstep. Alexander looked exhausted, his face haggard and shoulders tense. Without a second thought, Cece threw her arms around him to draw him inside. She led him to her sagging couch, wincing when the man's massive weight made the weak frame creak ominously. "So, how'd it go?"

"We've a long way to go." The District attorney drew his hands over his face before dragging his fingers through his hair, mussing the blonde strands. Though Cece knew he must be stressed, she couldn't help but gaze upon him fondly for a moment.

This was the man who had changed her life.

The man who did everything in his power to make the world a better place.

Her heart swelled with affection for him.

"Well, everyone has to start somewhere." She sank down on the couch beside him, cupping his face to draw it down to hers for a lingering kiss. "I know how hard this must be for you, Alexander. And I'm proud. Your mother would be too."

Alexander traced her lips briefly with his thumb before gazing over her shoulder at the new program she'd been watching. All at once, his body went absolutely taut. The man's very presence seemed to bristle and his eyes narrowed, his grip on her tightening almost to the point of pain.

Cece gasped, wincing at his hold on her arm. "Alexander, you're hurting me!"

But the man didn't let go.

After a moment, she turned to look at the television, and what she was made her blood run cold.

" - a mass fight in the upstate penitentiary caused by this man, one Jamal Thompson. The inmate was the perpetrator of a murder inside his cell block that led to riots that killed two guards and three additional prisoners." The breaking news bulletin flashed across the screen: MURDER AND RIOT AT UPSTATE NEW YORK PRISON. The newscaster continued speaking, but Cece, riveted by the images on the screen, didn't hear her.

The man whose face flashed behind the petite blonde was unmistakable.

He had scars, tattoos she'd never seen before, and it looked like his teeth were rotting over his mouth, but Cece would could never forget that face.

It haunted her nightmares.

"Dad."

The word escaped her on the barest of whispers. It seemed that her father still hadn't changed. All at once, the pain of her childhood, of being forced to run drugs and hunt for food in garbage cans after her mother died, everything rushed back to her. She remembered the first time she ever held Xaviar in her arms – how her father had refused to look at the infant. How he had scorned her and her brother and wanted to give him up for the government money he would bring.

That had been the last time she'd seen him.

Of course, she knew what had landed him in jail. She'd known he'd murdered, he'd stolen and he'd raped for his drug addiction. She'd spent her entire life trying to shield Xaviar from the man's influence.

This man in no way, shape or form resembled the one in the picture she'd saved.

But she knew him.

"What did you say?"

She gasped as Alexander's grip on her only tightened. She turned to see the man's narrowed gaze focused on her and her heart constricted at his expression.

She'd never seen such raw emotion on his face. "I...that's..." She took a shuddering breath. "That's my father. I...I told you he was in jail."

"*That's* your father?" Alexander's voice had taken almost a desperate edge. It seemed as if he was almost begging her to deny the words she'd just spoken, but Cece could no sooner take them back than she could change who she was. "*That* man?"

"Yes." She winced as his fingers dug into her arm. "Alexander, that *hurts*."

He finally released her, but as he did so, the man stood from the couch, placing distance between her and himself. The vivid red marks of his fingers stood out on her upper arm, and Cece stared at him, her heart in her throat. What the hell was wrong with him? Alexander would never hurt her – never allow himself to betray so much emotion so suddenly.

"That man, *Jamal Thompson*," Cross' words were uttered with such powerful hatred that she shivered, "is my mother's murderer."

Cece couldn't breathe.

The breath whooshed from her lungs and blood roared in her ears.

No. It couldn't be. It was *impossible.*

She knew that her father had be involved in a murder case that had landed him in jail when Xaviar was just a baby, but she didn't know many of the details. It had distressed her to watch the case, and so she had turned away from it, just as she'd turned away from her father.

But this...this was a nightmare.

Slowly, she shook her head. "Alexander, no...he couldn't be-"

"You think I don't know his face?" The man's words lashed out at her like a whip. "That it hasn't haunted my every waking moment since he took her from me?" The man turned from her, a low sound of frustration escaping him as he raked his hands through his hair.

Cece was numb. She couldn't believe it. How could they have been together in the ways that they had been...how could they have worked side by side for so long without knowing?

"Did you know?" At the demand, uttered in a low, dark timbre, Cece's mouth fell open. Had she known? How could she have possibly known? And if so, did he *really* think she'd be able to hide something of this magnitude from him?

"Alexander, I swear, I had no idea."

"*Fuck.*" The man uttered a curse that made her cringe. He almost never used profanity– but then again, he'd never looked at this way, his green eyes filled with pain, anger, and unmistakable betrayal. "How do you not know the name of the person your own father murdered?"

The words stung, cutting her to the quick. "You know I distanced myself from the man. I want nothing to do with him!"

"But everything to do with me? Your father *killed* my mother and now you expect me to go on as if nothing is different?"

"Alexander." Though she tried to keep her voice steady, it broke halfway through her plea. "You *know* me. I would never have lied to you about something like this. Wasn't it *you* who told me that you can't judge people by their ethnicity or parentage? I can't *choose* who my father is, but trust me, if I could, it would be *anyone* else."

"But it's *not*, Cecilia. It's Jamal fucking Thompson." Grabbing his coat, Alexander shook his head, as if trying to come to terms with the harsh reality laid out before him. "You're the daughter of a *murderer*. I brought you into my office, into my bed, and I almost...."

Tears sprang into Cece's eyes as the man emitted a frustrated sound, mussing his hair further. When his green eyes met hers, the intensity there was breathtaking.

She saw hatred.

Raw hatred.

So much like what she'd seen in Edward Cross' eyes that it took her breath away. Without a word, the man left her house, his scent and the power of his anguish lingering in his wake.

For a moment, all Cece could do was stare after him.

Her father...his mother...it was *her* family that had caused Alexander such pain. Her family that had created the stereotype that fueled his father's preconceptions.

Her hands shaking, the young woman brought them to her mouth.

Jesus. *Jesus.*

She glanced up at the TV again, and her father's image stared her in the face.

Challenged her.

She'd tried to run, tried to fight him – but in the end, he had come back to haunt her in a way she never would have expected, and stolen away the man she loved.

When the phone rang, she was shaking so badly that she dropped the receiver twice before she managed to lift it to her mouth. Her mind awhirl and her heart aching in her chest, she answered vacantly.

"Hello?"

"Ms. Thompson? Ms. Cecilia Thompson?"

She didn't recognize the curt, authoritative voice on the other line. "Yes...that's me."

"This is Officer John Kent of the NYPD. We need you to come down to the precinct. We have your brother in custody for possession of an illegal substance."

No.

No, no, no.

Righting Wrongs

The moment she hung up the phone, Cece raced upstairs to her bedside table where she'd stashed all the bills Xaviar had presented to her over the past few months. Dropping to her knees on the rough wooden floor, she hardly felt the pain. Cece yanked open the drawer, pulling out a handful of bills.

Frantically, she uncrumpled them, her eyes widening.

One, after another, after another.

They were not the fives and tens she had thought, but fifties and one hundreds. All in all, there was over three thousand dollars in hard bills in her drawer, and she sheer amount of money she held astounded her.

This was not the kind of money a teenager made selling candy.

It was clear that Xaviar had been selling something else.

At that point, Cece broke.

She usually considered herself a strong woman. She had weathered through her fair share of storms and come out strong. She didn't let her problems cow her, and she always grabbed the bull by the horns, but this was too much.

The man she loved couldn't see beyond her father's infamous name and her brother, upon whom her hopes for the future had rested, had already started following in his footsteps.

He had lied to her. They *both* had.

Sobbing, Cece shrank into herself, her forehead against the filthy floor as tears streamed down her cheeks. This was worse than losing her job, worse than any hunger pang, and worse than any grief she'd ever felt, however powerful.

Even from behind bars, her father still ruled her life, and she could be nothing more than a slave to his legacy.

When Cece went to the South Brooklyn precinct that evening, Jasmine was by her side. She'd barely been able to calm herself enough to tell her girlfriend what had happened, but as soon as she'd understood, the executive had rushed over.

The moment the entered the establishment, the smell of piss, sweat and aggression hit Cece like a ton loader. She made a beeline for the front desk, her eyes raw and red from her tears. "I'm here for Xaviar Thompson." The words came from her in a croak that was hardly recognizable.

The man on duty, however, seemed impervious to her grief. He merely stood, hitching up his belt, as he gestured for her to follow him. Jasmine squeezed her hand tightly as they wound their way through a plethora of young man, with sagging pants and golden teeth. Some of them tussled with the cops that held them while others just glared challengingly at them as they passed by. When one boy – who looked about half her age – had the nerve to hit on her from his position handcuffed to a desk, Cece could only stare back at him, horrified.

"It's ok, Cece. It's alright. Keep moving."

Jasmine's firm hand on her elbow steered her onward.

Righting Wrongs

But the cell block was no better. There were ten or fifteen young men to each cell, most of the ethnic. They gambled and scrapped and colored the air with profanity. Against her will, Cece was taken back to the days of her youth, where she'd encountered this kind of environment every day. This was what she'd wanted to protect Xaviar from – what she'd fought against all her life.

Her youngest brother was in the last cell, huddled against the bars. When Cece saw him, her tears began anew.

At the sound of her sobs, Xaviar turned. The boy's own eyes were red, his expression miserable. The sight of his sister made him redden as he pressed himself against the bars of his cell. "Cece...I'm sorry. I'm so sorry."

She clung to the bars to keep from falling, her knees weak beneath her. "I only wanted to make money, I swear. I wanted to help us get out of here."

It was *her* fault.

She'd driven him to this. Somehow, she hadn't been able to convey to him that their situation was getting better. She hadn't taught him enough patience. "Xaviar..." She took a shuddering breath, her eyes searching his. "What have I taught you? Drugs are never the answer. I'll find a way for us. I always do...Poisoning your body and mind like this...Christ, how could I have been so ignorant?" She should have watched him more closely.

Instead, she'd been too busy getting lost in Alexander Cross.

"Cece, I swear I never touched the stuff. Not a gram. I was only running for Malcolm. The money...I only wanted to help you. To help us. Cece...please get me out of here." Tears rose in the boys eyes and her heart seized in her chest. "I'm scared."

Cece immediately glanced back at the guard standing behind them. "When can I take him home? He's only fourteen."

In response, the man merely shook his head slowly, expression stoic. "Ma'am, this kid was caught with over a kilo of product on him. He'll have to make bail."

The breath whooshed from her lungs. A kilo? A kilo of *what*?

Thankfully, Jasmine came to her rescue, her grip firm on her friend's shoulder. "How much?"

"Five K."

Cece grasped at her companion, her breath hitching in shock. Five *thousand* dollars? For a fourteen year old boy? She'd heard that measures in South Brooklyn for drug offenders were steep, but this steep? "Do you have a lawyer? Because if you don't, the state will assign one to him."

How was she supposed to pay for a lawyer? If she scraped together all her resources, she might have *just* enough money to pay bail. Taking a deep breath, she tried to calm herself. Staring through the bars at her younger brother's face, Cece straightened her backbone.

The tiniest iota of hope still remained.

If what Xaviar said was true – that he had been running and not selling – perhaps she could somehow get the lawyer to speak to someone to make bargain for him.

Information brokering – of the kind she had always arranged for Alexander.

Righting Wrongs

Just thinking of him made the young woman nauseous, her chest tightening. Alexander wasn't here to help her now.

She was completely on her own.

Cristina Grenier

CHAPTER 9 - RIGHTING WRONGS

Two weeks.

Two weeks she hadn't come into work.

Alexander had seen neither hide nor hair of Cecilia since the day of the news bulletin in her apartment.

As much as he tried to concentrate on the cases he worked on, without his PA's help, organizing paperwork was complicated and tedious. It left him far too much time to think.

And think he did.

He thought about his father and the forceful way he'd struck out verbally at her in the manor. He thought of his mother's body lying cold on the kitchen floor before her fiftieth birthday. But most of all, he thought of Jamal Thompson, and how a woman like Cece could have come from such a monster.

He was angry. Angry that he hadn't discovered the truth for himself and angry for coming to feel the way he did about her. The depth of his emotions only made the realization a much more punishing blow.

The woman he loved was the daughter of the man he hated above all others.

Thompson should have gotten a life sentence. Hell, if it were up to Alexander, he should have gotten the electric chair. It wasn't fathomable that the man still lived and breathed – went on to murder others, while his mother was in her grave. He was pure evil incarnate.

That's why Cece broke with him.

The nasty little voice in the back of his head taunted him. *She told you she wanted nothing to do with him...spent her entire life trying to protect her brother from his influence.*

Or so she'd said.

Groaning, Alexander tossed aside the pen he'd been writing with, his thoughts tortured. He'd insulted her. He'd accused her and berated her...and for what?

For being related to a murderer? For something she couldn't help?

He'd seen cases like hers many times in his years as a lawyer. Individuals with vibrant lives and distinct personalities were relegated to simple titles. The axe murderer's widow, The rapist's son, the thief's daughter...their existences fell into the shadows of those that had done wrong and they could never escape.

Was that what had happened to Cecilia?

And if it was...could he ever come to terms with her parentage, and what her father had cost him?

He had no idea. What Alexander did know was that he missed her. He missed the scent of her perfume and the snide comments she leveled at him early in the morning. He missed the feel of her in his arms and the sight of her lovely face when she brought him his coffee.

It was idiotic of him, he knew, to expect that she'd continue to come to work in the wake of such a personal blow. They were too deeply involved, and he'd spoken too harshly. Knowing that she had walked out on him when she could least afford to added to his guilt.

What weight did his accusations really carry?

What was Cecilia guilty of?

His intercom rang, jerking him from his thoughts. Surprisingly, in his PA's absence, Margaret had done a rather good job of picking up the slack – at least when it came to running the office. With paperwork, she was still completely hopeless. "Yes, Margaret?"

"Mr. Cross, there's a call for you on the line. Shall I transfer it?"

"Who is it?"

"A Ms. Jasmine Saunders. She says its important that she speak with you."

Jasmine Saunders. The name sounded familiar. "Very well. Transfer the call."

His phone rang two seconds afterward and he picked up curtly. "This is Cross."

"Mr. Cross?" The voice that replied was low, husky, and undeniably feminine. "This is Jasmine Saunders. I'm a friend of Carol Mathers."

One of Carol's friends? He hadn't spoken to Carol since she'd passed on the recommendation that had led to his hiring Cecilia. At the memory, he frowned, his fist clenching. "What can I do for you Ms. Saunders?"

"You can listen." The agitation in the woman's voice was now very evident. When she spoke again, her words sent a chill down his spine. "Mr. Cross, I'm about to impart on you some very important information. What you chose to do with it is your own business, I just thought you had a right to know."

The large man bristled, his green eyes narrowing. "A right to know what?"

"What's happened with your employee, Cecilia Thompson."

Alexander's stomach immediately clenched in apprehension. What had...*happened* to Cecilia? What the hell was she talking about?

"Cece's brother was caught by the NYPD with a kilo of cocaine on his person, almost two weeks ago. They let the kid out on bail, having found no traces of drugs in his system, but he's set to go to trial in the next few days. South Brooklyn's pressing him hard, and the shit lawyer the state has pinned him with is trying to get him to settle for a plea bargain that will get him two years in juvenile detention." As he listened, Alexander's eyes grew wider and wider. Xaviar in jail? He'd been caught with *drugs*?

He didn't know the boy, but he couldn't picture it. He'd seemed like a good kid – and God knew Cecilia was a careful and doting parent. "If *someone* doesn't intervene, the boy's going to get put away and Cece will be devastated. She lives for the kid, and she's convinced he has information on the actual dealer himself. Everyone's too focused on convicting the poor boy to listen to her, so, things aren't looking to good for them now."

He could hardly believe what he was hearing.

All this had happened in the last two weeks?

In his opinion, if there was information Xaviar could give on real drug dealers, the situation should be taken advantage of. Why convict a misled boy when you could capture a whole ring? But smaller precincts didn't operate that way. They went heavy, and they went hard.

He knew this, and Cecilia certainly knew he knew it.

But she hadn't called him.

"Thank you for the information, Jasmine." He fought to keep his voice steady as he swallowed thickly.

"Cross, I want you to know that that woman has worked *hard* for everything she has. The only thing her father ever provided for her was misery and she's risen above it. In my opinion, you don't deserve her....but she still wants you."

The D.A's sharp retort died on his tongue.

Cece still wanted him?

After he'd slandered her name and accused her of siding with her father, and she still...

Alexander hung up the phone without a second thought. He had quite a few calls to make, and not very much time to make them in.

Two days later, he was at the courthouse at ten o'clock.

Xaviar's hearing was set for ten thirty, and he assumed that Cece and her brother would arrive early to speak with their lawyer.

He wasn't wrong.

When he caught sight of her face for the first time in almost three weeks, dark circles under her eyes and her mouth turned downwards, it took everything he had not to barrel through cops at her side and take her into his arms.

He wanted to kiss the pain away from her lovely mouth, even knowing that he had been its cause.

With Cece and Xaviar was another woman – an ebony-skinned stunner with her hair pulled back in a tight chignon. He could only assume that the woman was Jasmine Saunders, who'd told him off on the phone. She held Cece's hand tightly, as if supporting her companion, and Alexander's heart seized at the half-hearted smile Cece cast her.

He had done her grievous wrong.

Though the pain of his mother's death would never leave him, to accuse Cece of supporting a man who'd made her life a living hell just because they shared the same last name was unfair and cruel of him. He had stolen from her the support she needed in times like this, and the nastiness with which he'd cast her aside had almost cost her her brother's freedom.

But he would make sure that didn't happen.

Before he could lose his courage, Alexander strode across the entryway of the courtroom to meet the three halfway. When her gaze fell upon him, Cece stopped in her tracks, alarm flickering across her tired features. Jasmine was immediately on her guard at her side. "Mr. Cross." She nodded in greeting. Xaviar said nothing, merely tucked against his sister's side, his eyes dark and miserable.

"Jasmine. Xaviar...Cece."

When he said her name, the young woman shuddered visibly, her eyes sliding closed. "Cross." The distance of the title pained him. "We have a court date. I can't speak with you now."

Cristina Grenier

When she moved to step past him, her brother in tow, Alexander took hold of the young man's arm, making him jump as he stopped his progress. " Xaviar." The boy's eyes went wide as he drew the youth back to him, bending down slightly to face him. Before Cece could protest, he pressed on. "You ran these drugs for a dealer, did you not?"

Cece's brother nodded slowly, his expression confused. "If I asked, could you give me the name of this dealer? His information and who he sells to?"

The boy nodded again, his gaze darting back to his sister nervously before Alexander shook him slightly. "I need you to swear to me, and to your sister, that you never touched, nor will you *ever* touch illegal substances again."

"I-I swear." The boy stammered, quite obviously afraid. "I only wanted to help her! You worked her like a dog and I just wanted her to have a break, OK?"

The adamant conviction in the young man's tone was heartbreaking. Behind him, Cece wiped away tears as she took hold of the boy's shoulders, her expression resigned. "We have to *go* Cross."

"No." His answer was short and authoritative as his gaze locked with hers. "You'll wait here while Xaviar and I meet with the lawyer and the judge. The boy shouldn't have to go to court. It will be traumatizing and difficult for him. If you'll work with me, Xaviar," He now directed his words towards the boy, "we can get you out of this. But you have to be honest, and you can't hold back any details."

The young man's face was now beginning to shine with the first desperate rays of hope. "You're going to get me off?"

Righting Wrongs

"I'm going to make sure you stay out of jail." Alexander's tone punctuated his seriousness. "The rest will be up to you." With that, he looked to Jasmine, who was smirking slightly, and then Cece, who was gazing up at him, her expression unreadable. "Do I have your permission to take him?"

Slowly, she looked over her brother's young, vulnerable form. When Cece's eyes returned to his, they were firm with resolve.

She nodded curtly, once.

Taking Xaviar's arm, Alexander started towards the judge's office. It wouldn't be hard to make the man see the sense of the deal – and Cece would rest easy once her brother's criminal record was expunged.

The question was, could she ever forgive him for how he'd treated her?

He'd deal with the problem at hand, and then he'd tackle the far more intimidating task: Re-earning the love he'd so callously cast aside.

The meeting went like a dream. Not only was the judge amenable to Alexander's terms, but he apologized to Xaviar for what had happened to him, moved by his story. Within the hour, the boy had provided a list of names that would be used to bust several dealers at the school he attended, including his friend, Malcolm.

When he ran back out into the lobby, grinning and exhausted, to tell his sister the good news, Cece only clung to him, tears dripping down her cheeks. For a moment, Alexander watched them, his heart swelling in his chest.

How could he ever have doubted this woman, who loved so deeply and fought so passionately for those important to her. She had never failed him.

He only wished he could say the same of himself.

When Jasmine offered to take Xaviar home, Cece agreed. The boy looked dead on his feet – almost as much as she herself. However, when her friend left, Xaviar in tow, she suddenly seemed to realize that Jasmine her friend had left her alone with Alexander.

On the front steps of the courthouse, she faced him, her expression conflicted. "Thank you, for this." Her words came out carefully, as she gazed over his tall form. "It's a debt I can never repay, and I'm sure you know that."

Alexander swallowed thickly, nodding. "Xaviar is no criminal. He's too smart for that...and it's all thanks to you."

Running a hand through her messy curls, Cece looked away, obviously pained by the compliment. "Look, Alexander, I'm going to come in soon to get my things. I think it's pretty obvious that we can't work together any more, and I wouldn't want to jeopardize your work more than I already have. I know how important it is to you."

He just stared at her. It was clear that he had injured her deeply, and still, the woman maintained the diplomacy of a queen. She didn't curse him – didn't hurl insults. Instead, she merely looked into his eyes and offered to remove herself.

"Cece, you can't quit."

She gaped at him, disbelief evident at his words. Before she could say anything, however, the D.A continued quickly. "You keep talking about knowing what's important to me, but I'll tell you right now, I was idiotic enough to throw what's *most* important to me away for selfish reasons."

Her honey eyes widened as she stared at him with rapt attention. "I'm absolutely useless without you, both as a lawyer and as a man. I realize now that it doesn't matter who the hell your father is. *You* didn't pull that trigger. Here I am trying to teach my father that when I can't even get it straight. I hurt you, Cece, I know it. But, if you'll let me...I'll make things better."

For a moment, the city around them hummed and bustled as they stared at another, and Cece's eyes clouded with uncertainty a moment before she replied with a single word.

"How?"

Alexander took her in, from windswept curls to full mouth and intelligent eyes. "Well, to start with, I'll grovel." As she looked on in shock, he lowered himself to his knees before her to look up at her shapely form. "I'll beg. I know I don't deserve you, but I want you, and I'll do whatever it takes."

Cece's cheeks flushed as she glanced around at the plethora of people staring at them. "Alexander, get up!" Her words were whispered frantically. "What are you doing?"

He ignored her, taking a slender hand between both of his as he continued dramatically. "Then I'll force you to move out of that rat trap duplex and into my townhouse. I'll make sure both you and Xaviar are fed until your bursting every night. I'll pay for him to go to the best school that money can buy and I'll prove to you every day for the *rest* of your life how lucky I am to have you...if you let me."

Cristina Grenier

Cece was scarcely breathing. As she stared down at him, moisture gleamed in her eyes.

"I...I can't take all of those things. I'll work. I'll earn my keep. I -"

"You'll depend on *me* because I *love* you, Cecilia. You've worked hard enough, and I think I've decided to fire you after all."

She leapt into his arms, her breath hitching with joyous sobs. "You can't fire me. You wouldn't last a day....and I love you too."

While Alexander had never been one for crying women, this was the one exception. He knew he'd better savor it, because if he was going to deal with Cece for the rest of her life, there would be far more stubbornness and arguments then there would be tears.

And he would relish every moment of it.

ABOUT THE AUTHOR

Hello,

So this is the part where I'm supposed to talk about myself. I write so many stories but I often I have a hard time telling my own. Funny how that works.

My name is Cristina Grenier and I have been writing stories for as long as I could remember . I'm a sucker for romance. I draw from past experiences and from others around me when I write. I enjoy creating characters that everyone can relate to.

Besides writing, I also enjoy painting and figure drawing. I'm a bit of a homebody, my ideal night consists of a chilled bottle of wine, some pasta and Netflix. I really hope you enjoy the stories I create.

If you enjoyed this title and want to keep updated with my new releases and frequent FREE book giveaways, please visit my website and submit your email.

Sincerely,

Cristina

www.cristinagrenier.com

CPSIA information can be obtained at www.ICGtesting.com
Printed in the USA
LVOW10s1545070415

433608LV00002B/637/P